D0192818

395365

OUTSIDE THE WHITE LINES

Chris Simms

OUTSIDE THE WHITE LINES

HUTCHINSON
London

To the memory of Ali Muir

Thanks to Christine for making it all possible

Published by Hutchinson in 2003

1 3 5 7 9 10 8 6 4 2

Chris Simms has asserted his right under the Copyright, Designs and
Patents Act 1988 to be identified as the author of this work.

This book is sold subject to the condition that it shall not, by way of trade or otherwise, be
lent, resold, hired out, or otherwise circulated without the publisher's prior consent in any
form of binding or cover other than that in which it is published and without a similar
condition including this condition being imposed on the subsequent purchaser

First published in the United Kingdom in 2003 by Hutchinson

Hutchinson
The Random House Group Limited
20 Vauxhall Bridge Road, London SW1V 2SA

Random House Australia (Pty) Limited
20 Alfred Street, Milsons Point, Sydney
New South Wales 2061, Australia

Random House New Zealand Limited
18 Poland Road, Glenfield
Auckland 10, New Zealand

Random House (Pty) Limited
Endulini, 5A Jubilee Road
Parktown 2193, South Africa

The Random House Group Limited Reg. No. 954009

www.randomhouse.co.uk

A CIP record for this book is available from the British Library

Papers used by Random House are natural, recyclable products made from
wood grown in sustainable forests. The manufacturing processes conform to
the environmental regulations of the country of origin

Typeset by SX Composing DTP, Rayleigh, Essex
Printed and bound in Great Britain by Clays Ltd, St Ives Plc

ISBN 0 0917 9538 9

318240

Prologue

As the tiny voice began to speak another huge lorry thundered past. Spray-laden swirls swept around his lower legs, flattening damp trousers against his shins. 'I'm sorry, I didn't catch that,' the man said.

Patiently the voice resumed. 'I said, try and get your head right into the telephone casing. It will cut out a lot of background noise.'

He did as he was asked and instantly appreciated the advice as the voice clearly said, 'Can you hear me better now?'

'Yes, much,' he replied and stopped pressing the telephone receiver quite so hard against the gristle of his ear.

'OK, sir, could you tell me what number is on the inside of the door?'

He angled his head to the side and read out the luminous white number.

There was a pause then the voice said, 'Right – so you're just beyond junction 14?'

He didn't know, but trusting whatever information the voice had to hand replied, 'Yes, that sounds about right.'

The voice then went on to ask him various questions about his vehicle, before finishing with, 'OK, sir, have you got breakdown cover with any motoring organisation?'

'I have,' he answered, and pre-empting the next question continued, 'Shall I read out my membership details?'

'Please.'

He held the card down at arm's length, and using the orange flash of his hazards read out four numbers with each blink of light.

Drips from the telephone casing fell steadily on to the back of his head as his details were processed. While waiting he reflected on his situation, stranded in the middle of the night on a deserted and unlit stretch of motorway. There was no way he was getting any more than a couple of hours' sleep before work the next day. Today, in fact, since morning was now only a few hours off. He felt frustrated at the way his car's failure had also rendered him completely powerless; up until now he'd always been one of the warm and cosy drivers speeding past the dark, cold cars parked on the hard shoulder. Suddenly he appreciated just why these telephones were called SOS points: no one stops to help on a motorway.

He'd counted 127 flashes of his hazards before the voice spoke to him again. 'OK, sir – you're down as a priority case, so a van should be with you in just under an hour. I know the conditions are bad tonight but I must advise you and your passenger to remain outside your vehicle, preferably well clear of it and up the grass verge.'

'Right, thanks for your help, is that everything?' he asked.

'Yes,' the voice replied. 'Of course, if there's no sign of any van after an hour feel free to call us again.' The line clicked dead.

'Thanks,' he said, feeling strangely vulnerable now the voice had gone. He replaced the receiver on the blank grey telephone, shut the little orange door and stepped back towards his car. With one hand on the roof, he looked through the rear passenger window at his sleeping daughter. Way off to his right, lights began to pierce the darkness. Squinting into the rain, he watched them grow in strength until a lorry rumbled past, rocking the car beneath his hand. To his relief she stayed fast asleep in the booster seat. Moving her outside the car was ridiculous, he thought, glancing uneasily at the, for now, empty lanes. Guiltily, he climbed into the front passenger seat and quietly pulled the door shut. The dashboard clock read 3.18 a.m.

Coarse blades of wet grass poked into his face, the tiny serrations on their edges making a virtually imperceptible rasp on the skin of his cheek. On rainy nights like this the moisture seemed to free the acrid deposits from exhausts trapped in the greenery around him. Even though the smell made his nostrils itch and smart, he resisted the temptation to wipe his sleeve across his nose because he knew it would remove the carefully applied camouflage cream coating his face. Barely twelve feet from his head a car raced past, wet tyres hissing on the tarmac, headlights flickering between the crash barrier's struts like an ancient cinema projector. He wondered if the grass could have drawn blood.

Pushing his left forearm out he bent the clump backwards, and keeping himself perfectly flat wriggled over the top. Beyond, a dip in the ground offered improved cover and he inched his body forward into the depression. As he did so his elbow knocked against a can. He stopped moving at the hollow metallic noise. Fingers probed the vegetation until the object was located. Holding it in front of his face, he used his other hand to twist the pencil torch gripped in his teeth. Insulation tape over its end reduced the beam to laser-like proportions. Using his tongue he played the pinpoint of light over the metal surface: a standard Coke can, not even from outside the EU. He discarded it, turned the torch off and then lay motionless for a while with his eyes shut, waiting for his night vision to return.

He relished these visits more than anything else in his life. This was his territory, free from any other humans through their very proximity within hurtling metal cages. He imagined the unkempt stretches of grass on the central reservations to be islands and the motorway lanes surrounding them an impenetrable grey moat. This was his little kingdom, shared only with the vermin, scavengers and foraging creatures of the night. He knew they also came here because he'd find their pathetically smeared remains where they'd tried to cross back over the hard expanse of tarmac into the normal countryside beyond. Field-mice, dormice, voles, shrews, hedgehogs, weasels, rats and stoats – he'd collected all manner of corpses, or what was left of them after the cars had crushed them and the crows had taken their pick.

Another vehicle shot past, this time on his right-hand side, going in the opposite direction. By now the rain had begun to soak through his army surplus all-in-one suit. He wondered how much searching he had left before it started getting light. Opening his eyes he craned his head back, looking for any sign of the full moon. He wasn't able to see the unbroken cloud covering the sky, just sense its weight in the blackness above. Reluctantly he undid the Velcro clasp on his cuff and glanced at the luminous-tipped hands of his watch: they read 3.21 a.m.

The driver's window suddenly hummed into life, destroying the peace that had slowly settled over the two occupants. As glass slid into door, cold air and spatters of rain immediately began blowing in. He looked questioningly at the man slouched before the steering wheel, hands resting on his paunch.

'I'd lower yours too – I've just dropped one.'

'Jesus,' he replied, scrabbling in the dark before the first whiffs hit him.

'This,' the driver announced, 'is going to be a right shag of a night. Pissing rain and stinking wind – I wouldn't be in your shoes on this shift.' He popped the last two tablets from a blister pack and tossed the empty sheet of plastic through the open window. 'Bloody indigestion,' he said, swallowing the two pills. 'Do you know, I have to sleep sitting up in bed? It's the only way of stopping the acid from burning the back of my throat.'

The passenger grimaced in sympathy and poked his nose into the cold stream of air coming through the gap in his window. The driver stared out of the motionless police car's windscreen and drummed his fat fingers on the steering wheel. Suddenly the radio spat static and a buzzing voice said, 'Base to 1820F4, RTA involving two vehicles reported off the slip road at junction 8, northbound. Please attend.'

The response came almost immediately. '1820 to base, will be at the scene in about six minutes.'

'Roger 1820. Be advised a member of the public has already called for an ambulance.'

The younger man listened intently. Four days into his attachment and he still couldn't make out half of what was being said over the car radio.

'Well, that's bog-all to do with us – and it's too far to go just to give you a bit of roadside experience, son,' said the driver, closing his window. 'I reckon we'll go and get a coffee at the services. I could do with a dump and all.'

'Aren't we meant to be checking on all breakdowns at the moment, Sarge?' asked the passenger.

The driver glanced disdainfully across at the car marooned on the opposite hard shoulder. 'Yeah – but we'll check on him later. I can't be shagged driving to the next exit and coming all the way back now.'

Not waiting for his passenger to respond, he started the engine and turned on the lights. The patrol car rolled slowly down the concealed ramp on to the hard shoulder and pulled away. As they moved off the younger man watched the flashing hazard lights from the car on the other side of the motorway slowly disappear. When the 'Services 8 miles' sign drifted lazily past he glanced at the dashboard clock: 3.26 a.m.

'Too many bastard cars,' he cursed to himself. Forced to take the M25 at rush hour he'd crawled round it at little more than walking pace. With every click of his dashboard clock more money had escaped him. He thought of the brown envelopes with their machine-gun type and angry red demands gathering back home and then strained his eyes looking ahead – but there were only cars in front; no gaps, no way through.

Trapped there he'd scrutinised other drivers in the lanes alongside as they sat, motionless and resigned, watching with glazed eyes as their lives slipped slowly by. Almost all were selfish wankers who, if they weren't so lazy, could easily have found an alternative way into work. Did none of them live near a fucking train station? The only sympathy he had was for fellow drivers like himself. Vans, trucks, lorries – people using the roads for proper work purposes. Not like these twats, alone in their cars, sat on their fat arses and getting in his way.

When he'd finally got off the M25 and on to the M26, he'd been able to put his foot down a bit. Feel more in control. He'd smilingly taken out a couple of crows pecking at something dead on the hard shoulder. The vulture-like bastards never expected a vehicle to jink across the white lines; too late they struggled into the air, ragged wingtips clawing desperately at the flat sky. Puff. He'd turned them into broken balls of black feathers. No doubt their mates were on the carcasses in minutes.

But finding the garage where he was dropping the components off had then taken ages too. After that came the paperwork. And so here he was, making the return trip halfway through the frigging night, having made piss-all from the job. The fury had built in him all day and now it constricted his chest like a giant tubi-grip. He bit on the last piece of banana then unwound his window and hurled the skin out. As soon as it crossed the window frame the roar snatched it, sending it flapping through the air on to the central reservation.

Bollocks, he decided. Even if it was pouring with rain he needed some sport, and the bad weather only increased his chances of success. He pulled his van into the approach road for the services then, avoiding the feeder lanes luring him to the welcoming glow of the restaurant car park, carried round on a smaller, unlit service road to the rear of the buildings. Pulling up in the shadows, he jumped from the van and slid back the side door. From a hold-all he removed a grey boiler suit and neon waist jacket and put them on. Then he took out a torch, magnetic siren light, and tool-box containing a heavy-duty monkey wrench. Placing it all on the front passenger seat, he restarted the engine and, in seconds, was back on the motorway system searching for prey.

The steady blink of hazard lights let him know of the stranded vehicle long before he could actually see it. Instantly he slowed and checked in his rear-view mirror that the road behind was still deserted. Then he unwound the window and placed the magnetic siren light on the cab roof before switching it on. Waves of adrenaline surged through his thick arms as the yellow flashes of the lamp began revolving above him. He eased smoothly on to the hard shoulder, and, as he crossed the white line, the ridges made a sharp drilling noise through his tyres. He dropped his speed still further and stopped fifteen feet behind the solitary car.

Its passenger door opened and a man got out. With one hand he shielded his eyes from the glare of the van's lights, with the other he made a kind of awkward salute. Darts of rain flashed through the headlights in a steady flow. The van driver sat motionless. From behind his dark windscreen he scanned the interior of the car for the silhouettes of any other heads. Seeing none a delicious rush played up his spine. Flicking his headlights off and hazards on, he jumped eagerly from the van and grabbed the torch and toolbox.

Confidently he strode up to the man with his first line ready prepared, but the car driver cut in first.

'Great to see you! I wasn't expecting you for at least another half-hour or so.'

That was his first question answered: no rescue van due for a while. He cut straight to the next part of his speech. 'You're in luck, mate. All the regular vans are busy with this bad weather. So they've sent me from a garage down the road.'

'Oh, right, I wondered why there were no logos and things painted on your vehicle. I'm still covered for any repairs, though?'

'Oh, yeah, pal, 'course,' he replied, quickly walking round to the front of the car. 'Let's get it sorted and you on your way.'

'Superb. The bonnet's already popped.'

'Cheers,' the van driver replied, already disliking the man's eager politeness. He secured the bonnet with the metal arm and turned his torch on. The beam cut across the top of the engine, throwing wires and tubes into stark relief and creating exaggerated shadows between the engine parts behind. He needed the driver right by him and not standing off to the side like some spare part. 'Right, what was the problem again, sir?' he called over while starting to pull gently at the spark plugs.

The car driver glanced at him and then stepped to within talking distance. 'Well, as I outlined to the phone operator, I thought I was running out of petrol at first. The needle started dropping but then so did all the power. Nothing too sudden – I was able to pull up right next to the phone, but now the engine's totally dead.'

'Mmmm. OK, could you keep the torch pointed right on that spot, sir?' the van driver asked. The man had to bend forward right into the jaws of the opened bonnet. Casually the van driver removed the monkey wrench from the tool-box at his feet, and with a quick glance to check no traffic was approaching, said in a voice pinched with excitement, 'Great, hold it right there, sir.'

With a sharp chopping motion, he brought the wrench down on the back of the man's skull. It gave way with a muffled crack and he fell forward on to the edge of the bonnet, torch dropping into the engine, beam pointing wildly off to the side. Before he could slide back, the van driver grabbed him by the belt, and with one arm heaved him easily off the engine so he dropped on to the tarmac by the side of the car.

Quickly the other man stepped around the vehicle, placed a foot on either side of his victim's outstretched legs, and crouched down so he was hidden from any passing traffic. He knew dispatching someone wasn't a quick and clean job, like it was in the films. But he'd expected at least some slurred begging, some groggy attempts at fending off the wrench as he smashed it into the face. That was how it had gone with the other two. But this one was just trying to wriggle back towards his car door. Did he really think he could find safety there?

He watched, fascinated, as the man frantically struggled to raise himself up on to his elbows. The blow to the back of his head must have split the skin – blood was flowing from his hair, coursing down his neck. Bending forwards, he looked over the prostrate man's shoulder and saw drips falling steadily off his nose and chin. He placed a knee on the man's buttocks to pin him down and then playfully batted the wrench across the side of his head. It jerked to one side and the skull itself shifted shape. The wounded man sagged back on to his stomach, then slowly started trying to edge forward again. And he began mumbling a name. Laura? Lauren? Probably calling for his fucking mum.

He shook his head in disgust, switched the wrench to his left hand and cracked him across the other side of his skull. The plates of his skull parted properly this time and a membranous lump began bulging through. That stopped his snivelling. He lay still now, except for one hand clawing frantically at the tarmac. The rasping of his nails was his last ever sound as, more firmly this time, the van driver brought the cast-iron tool down on the top of his head and watched as flabby bits of grey jelly tumbled out over his collar. The body began its nervous twitching, so he stood back up. Next he snatched his torch from the car's hard innards, lowered the bonnet back down and retrieved his tool-box. He stepped round the side of the car and played the beam of light over the man's head. It lay ruined in an oil slick of blood.

'Fucking ignorant prick,' he murmured, taking the first step back towards his van.

The small white face stared at him from behind the glistening window, pads of little fingers pressed against the glass. The van driver froze mid-step, and their eyes locked. In that instant before conscious thought, terrible realisations passed between them. A microsecond later and the van driver's elation had vanished.

His brain slowed and then began to stall, desperately trying to work out what to do. Secretly knowing the answer already. Realising he had to get moving, he snapped the rear door open, unclipped her harness and plucked her from the car. She didn't make a sound, just kicked her little legs in the air.

Bundling her into the passenger footwell of the van, he sprang across into the driver's seat, unaware of one of her shoes lying on the ground by the van's front tyre. No headlights approaching from behind. He grabbed the siren light off the roof, started the engine and crossed back on to the motorway lanes.

He sat slumped back in his plastic chair, one hand rotating an empty styrofoam cup on the cigarette-singed formica surface, the other turning an unopened sugar sachet end over end over end.

Opposite sat his young colleague, hands folded in his lap, trying not to look bored. Under the table his forefinger and thumb plucked like a vindictive chicken at the skin of his other palm. Black windows pressed in on all sides, reflecting back the interior lights, making the café feel smaller. In the kitchen behind them a radio quietly sounded the four o'clock pips.

The older man abruptly blew out his cheeks and glanced at his watch. 'Well, suppose we'd better make a move,' he announced, reaching for his cap on the seat beside him.

'Cheers for all the advice, Sarge,' the younger man replied, straightening his shoulders.

'No problem. You need to know the ins and outs of how the game's played. But like I told you, say anything to certain people and it goes straight . . .'

The handset on the table between them burst into life as a voice announced, 'All units in the vicinity of junction 14 on the M40, we have a report from a motorway assistance vehicle of a body next to a broken-down vehicle, east-bound hard shoulder. No other vehicles involved. Please respond.'

'Shit. That's us, come on,' said the driver, struggling to slide his gut out from under the bolted-down table. 'Not a word about us being in here, all right?' he said, once they were outside and marching across the car park. 'Roger base, driver 1214F4 responding, ten minutes away.'

'Junction 14, where's that from here?' the younger man asked as they pulled out of the car park and on to the roundabout, heading for the eastbound turn-off.

'Just about opposite where we were sat half an hour ago.'

'We saw that car!' he shouted excitedly. 'No other vehicles involved. What do you reckon?'

'Exactly – he's done it again.' The driver paused for a moment, then added, 'And Andy?'

'Yeah?' he replied eagerly.

'Calm the fuck down.'

With eyes shut, he remained absolutely motionless, relying totally on his sense of hearing. On his right the sound of the siren reached a painful peak as it passed his head. And then it was receding, suddenly growing fainter like some stereo effect heard in a giant cinema. His eyelids opened a fraction. At first he could see no difference but, as they widened, the broad leaves of dandelions showed their black outlines against the fractionally lighter sky. He began pressing forward again, nostrils flared for any unusual aromas. Sometimes he'd find the boxed and rotting remains of pizza slung on to his land. He'd pore over the mouldy lumps with his torch and note down the number of the shop. Once he'd rung one from a call-box and listened to the voice repeatedly asking for an order before eventually it hung up on him.

The sound of the siren still hadn't completely evaporated into the night air. He estimated he had another hour of foraging before dawn began to break. Time enough to cover a couple of hundred metres more. Just as well, he thought, since tonight had only produced two items worth adding to his collection. The siren now seemed to be coming back. He concentrated on the sound and then realised it was another, approaching from the same direction as the first. He closed his eyes once again and settled flat on to his stomach, head slightly up, ears clear of the soaking grass. The second siren passed him and from its tone he knew it was a different type of emergency vehicle. With the first one never having fully faded away, it was time to call off the forage.

He hated the end of his searches, when he was forced to lift himself from his belly and resume his existence on two feet. He hated leaving the debris that littered his territory like so much rubbish washed up on a deserted beach. Regretfully he returned the pencil torch to the zip-up pocket on the upper arm of his overalls, then, favouring his left elbow and knee, he burrowed off to the side until the crash barrier loomed above his head.

From the gap below the lowest strip of metal he peered out to his left. Twin points of approaching light caused him to shrink back into the shadows. A few seconds later the white van hurtled by, easily doing over a hundred. He glimpsed the crop-haired driver crouched over the wheel, willing the vehicle to go even faster.

He waited for a bit, then, looking again, saw the lanes were empty. Far beyond the motorway's gentle curve, the faint flicker of blue lights pulsed. Checking that the lanes behind him were also deserted, he quickly vaulted over the barrier and scuttled, legs stiff and crab-like, across the tarmac strip. Reaching the hard shoulder he didn't slow down, climbing the grassy slope in quick strides until he reached the edge of the field at the top. Glancing back at the central reservation, he resolved to return and complete his search of this particular stretch another time. And then he was over the fence and away into the night.

Chapter 1
The Hunter

'OK, everyone, quieten down, will you?'

The murmur of voices died away and faces looked to the front of the meeting room.

'As you all know there's been a third person killed last night – same circumstances as the other two, with one important difference I'll get to in a moment. Now, we haven't got evidence yet to confirm it's the work of the same person or persons, but until we uncover anything to suggest otherwise we're assuming it is. Which means we're now expecting this to carry on until we make an arrest.' He paused. 'In other words, ladies and gents, we've got a complete head-case out there, roaming the motorways and attacking people almost at random.'

His voice had paused again before the word 'almost' and bowed heads bobbed up at the emphasis he placed on the word.

'I say "almost" because there is a common thread so far to the attacks and that's all we've got to go on. All three victims were night breakdowns, on unlit stretches of the hard shoulder, and all three were male drivers. Which leads me to the major difference I mentioned before.

'First two victims were travelling alone. Last night's had a passenger. It seems his four-year-old daughter – Laura – was travelling with him; no sign of her at the scene except for one shoe found about fifteen feet behind the car. We're talking to the mother – she's divorced from the victim – and she says he was returning the girl home from some sort of event on his side of the family. She's correctly described the shoe, so the immediate area has been searched by a tracker dog. No sign of the child, which means she was probably transferred to another vehicle and so could be anywhere by now. Since previous attacks were on lone males, we're not sure if this one will turn out to be linked but let's assume for the moment it is.'

He looked down at his clipboard to find his place.

'Right, geographically speaking you might as well shut your eyes and throw three darts at a map of Britain. First one on the A1 just north of Scotch Corner. Second, M5 between Taunton and Exeter, and last night's – right on our patch, junction 14 of the M40. All three victims had made a call from the emergency roadside phone and were waiting for the rescue vehicle to arrive. Two were registered with the AA, the other with the RAC. Scotland Yard is already going through everyone who's worked as a motorway rescue driver in the last five years. However since there's –' he glanced at the clipboard '– currently around 3,500 AA drivers, 2,000 RAC drivers, over 6,000 Green Flag mechanics and God knows how many other independent garage drivers affiliated to those three, we're not expecting any quick answers from that search if they're left to do it all on their own. Which is where we – the cavalry – come in.

'Initially we're going to be helping out by running checks on any possible local suspects thrown up by the Yard's analysis of employment records in this area. That means paying visits to garages and the like where ex-rescue vehicle drivers are working. Every other motorway traffic division in the country is also stepping up patrols, running extra marked and unmarked cars on all night shifts. So yes, your rotas are being rejigged and we'll all be claiming nice fat chunks of overtime. We can also expect some help from the city traffic divisions, numbers to be confirmed. Setting up decoy breakdowns has been suggested as well – but this country has got around 7,000 miles of motorway and other major roads.'

He raised his eyebrows and took a deep breath.

'Basically we're looking for a needle in a haystack here until we get forensics, witnesses, etcetera. Any questions so far?'

A voice sounded from somewhere near the back of the room. 'Any footage from roadside cameras?'

'It's being looked at, but take last night's incident. From where the attack took place, the next set of cameras is at junction 19 where the motorway lighting resumes. There's four junctions he could have used to exit the motorway from before that.

'One more thing. The late edition of the local paper carried a paragraph in its "Stop Press" column – the incident's now been picked up by all the nationals, so get ready for this becoming the summer's big story. Details of the new shift rotas will be posted later today. Until then, that's it. Sergeant Walker and . . . your partner, can I see you both now?'

Everyone in the room rose to their feet and people started milling towards the doors. Obscured from the Inspector's sight, Walker used the opportunity to whisper to the younger man, 'Remember what we said, and let me do the talking.'

They wound their way between their dispersing colleagues, Walker grunting the odd 'morning' to a few of the older ones. Inspector Marsh half-sat with the edge of the desk digging into his buttocks, arms folded and clipboard tucked under one armpit.

'OK, Ray, and – sorry, I don't know your name?'

'Constable Andy Seer, sir.' He winced at the clash of words.

'Good. Now, Ray – God, you look like you've been up all night – oh yes, you have.' He grinned at his joke. Walker chuckled back, and Seer, taking his cue from the other two men, broke into an uncertain smile. 'You didn't see anything out there tonight?'

Walker quickly replied, 'Unfortunately not, sir. Our patrol covered the stretch the attack took place on, but we were positioned about eight miles away at the time of the incident on the flyover by the Granada services.'

'None of the eastbound traffic caught your attention?'

'No – but we were positioned observing traffic going west. The eastbound lanes were actually behind us.'

'OK. It's a shame – you were so close. Well, Constable Seer,' he said as he pushed himself off the edge of the desk, 'I bet this has been a bit of a rude introduction to the job. Still keen on making a career out of motorway traffic police?'

'Yes, sir,' His answer felt too short so he awkwardly added, 'Absolutely.'

'Excellent. Well, the new rotas will be up this afternoon – expect to be spending a lot more time together.' He headed out of the room, leaving them alone.

Walker looked at his colleague. 'Well done – you played that all right.'

Andy replied, voice kept low, 'I didn't like keeping quiet – I wanted to tell him that at least we'd seen the broken-down car on the other side of the motorway.'

'Listen, mate,' Walker hissed, jowls wobbling slightly as he leaned close, 'so what? You glimpsed the car. Nothing more. It's of no consequence, so just drop it.'

'Yeah, but – I'm caught up now, aren't I? In your . . . dishonesty.'

'Oh, for fuck's sake, if you think getting on in this job has got anything to do with honesty you've got a lot to learn.'

'What's that supposed to mean?' Andy whispered.

Walker looked into his bright young eyes and a wave of weariness almost made him sit down. 'That you've got a lot to learn, that's what.'

'Yeah?' said Andy indignantly. 'And I reckon that attitude is why you're reporting to people ten years younger than yourself.'

The comment cut deeper than he could possibly realise. Walker looked out of the corner of his eye at the novice who had just dismissed his entire career – who had just dismissed his entire career accurately – with hatred. He screwed the lid down on the well of venom rising inside him and instead stated flatly, 'I'm knackered. We should have clocked off hours ago. I'm going home.'

He puffed his way out of the room, leaving Andy staring angrily out of the window at the watery morning sky.

Chapter 2
The Killer

'Shut her up, will you? I can't concentrate on this.'

Steam billowed from the boiling kettle as the woman attempted to spoon formula powder into a bottle with one hand while jiggling the crying baby on her hip with the other. The water bubbled louder and louder. He glanced at the kettle, at his wife, at the kettle again, before letting out an elongated 'Christ' through clenched teeth. He reached over and turned it off.

'When did you get in, babe?' she asked over her shoulder.

'About half a frigging hour ago.'

'I didn't hear you come in. Was the traffic bad again?'

'Traffic bad? Next delivery I get for down London way, I'm going to tell Clarke if it's not in the morning, it isn't even worth me setting off. The whole bastard area is one big traffic jam. I'll have made fuck-all on that job.'

He snapped the morning paper open to create a barrier between himself and the room. The crying continued for another minute before he heard a chair scrape back and felt the table jar as his wife sat down. Abruptly the crying stopped, and was replaced by sucking sounds.

'Make us a tea, will you, darling?' she asked from beyond his paper.

'Lay off, will you, Sal? I just want to read this and get some sleep.'

Air bubbles percolated into the milk bottle as the baby took a break from feeding.

'Oh, God, look.' Her voice had gone high. 'Someone else has been killed on the motorway. Whereabouts was it?'

He glanced over the top of the paper to see her leaning across the table trying to read the 'Stop Press' column on the back page facing her.

'For fuck's sake – you're squashing Jasmine.'

She quickly leaned back, glancing down at the baby cradled in her lap. He swiftly closed the paper, so the back page was facing him. 'I tell you, Selkirk is two more defeats away from getting binned as manager of City.'

'You be careful when you're on the motorways – I don't want you getting attacked.'

Slowly he lowered the paper. 'Listen, who's going to jump me if I don't break down? I look after my motor. It's only losers who can't fix their own engine that are getting topped.'

'Well, just be careful, Dave. You're on the motorway at all hours, and it worries me.'

He got up to break the conversation.

'What are you doing today?' he asked, lining up two cups in front of the kettle.

'Oh,' she said, her voice brightening. 'I'm taking Jasmine round to her gran's and we're going to the Clearwater Centre for some shopping.'

'More shopping?' he said, with exaggerated surprise.

'Sod off, Dave – I've had nothing for ages, and you know it. What are you up to – have you got any more work on?'

'There might be a local delivery later this afternoon,' he said, flicking a teabag into the sink. 'But I'm meeting Jeff at the gym for twelve-thirty, so right now I'm going to bed.'

As he put her cup of tea on the table, he bent down and kissed the top of the baby's head. 'Night, dolls,' he said, sauntering out of the tiny kitchen, paper tucked under his arm. But as soon as he was round the corner, his jaw clenched tight.

Chapter 3
The Searcher

He knew people watched him, hidden behind their musty, yellowed netting, angled with one eye on the lit box, the other on the street.

That's why, when he got back to his car after any forage, he followed a strict routine before setting off home. Changing out of his overalls, he'd stash everything in the space below the boot that was supposed to contain the spare tyre. Next he'd transfer any trophies into plain white boxes and place them in crisp, unused supermarket shopping bags on the back seat. Then he'd take out the baby wipes from the glove box and, using the car's interior light, scrupulously remove all camouflage cream from his face and hands. Next he'd remove from his person any burrs, twigs or other fragments from the central reservation itself, and comb his hair. Then he'd drive back along whatever lane or farm-track he'd left his car on for the forage, rejoin the main road and slip back on to the motorway – always just a few fields from where he'd originally parked.

Now, pulling up outside his house, he took a deep breath and climbed out of his car. Further down the road an electric motor whirred to a stop and bottles clinked as the milkman ferried fresh ones up to a front door. Keeping his eyes firmly averted from the windows all around him, he walked briskly round the vehicle, opened the side passenger door and removed the shopping bag with his right hand, locked the door with his left and turned quickly on his heel. As he walked up the short path to his front door he let the car key drop from his fingers and slide round the key ring. With his forefinger and thumb he selected his front door key and, extending it in front of him, reached towards the door. Key turned smoothly in lock and he stepped into the cool, dim hallway beyond, immediately shutting the door behind him. Only once the lock actually clicked could he empty his lungs in a slow whoosh and breathe in again.

His house smelt.

It was a curious smell and one that would remind many police officers of biology lessons and the aroma of dead animals pickled in jars. Striding up the narrow corridor he walked straight past the first room (reserved for 'genus of flora and other plant life'), past the second (reserved for 'items of a biodegradable nature thrown from vehicles'), and into his kitchen/examination room. Harsh fluorescent lighting flickered into life.

He placed the shopping bag on the bare formica-topped table and proceeded immediately to the kitchen drawers. From the third one down he removed a tray filled with assorted laboratory instruments and returned to the table. As he slid the chair out it shuddered slightly on the linoleum floor.

He sat.

The shopping bag rustled as he removed the two white boxes. Gently opening the lid of the first, he looked inside. The withered remains of the driver's glove huddled in the corner like a frightened animal. Taking a large pair of tweezers from the tray he carefully lifted it out, turning it around, examining it for any interesting features. Gold writing on the back caused his wrist to stop rotating. *'Fabbricato in Italia, geniuno pelle.'*

Interesting. If the glove had been intended for the export market it seemed likely that at least *'geniuno pelle'* would have been written in English. This meant the glove had not only originated in Italy, but was probably also from a car that had travelled from that country. It merited a place in his collection. He considered for a moment if it should be placed in the room reserved for 'items of a biodegradable nature' – after all, dead animal skin was surely that. However, on reflection, he decided that it had undoubtedly been treated with preserving agents, and so decided instead to place it in the upstairs room reserved for 'items of a non-biodegradable nature thrown from vehicles'.

Dropping the glove back into its box, he slid that to one side and selected the other. His fingers hovered momentarily above it like a pianist's before deftly flicking the lid open.

The dead dragonfly lay with wings outspread, leaning to one side like a stricken World War I biplane. An initial glance revealed only minor damage to its abdomen, none to its thorax or head, and a slight crumpling in one of the lower wings which was causing its unbalanced posture. With extreme care he used a pair of surgical tweezers to lift the insect out by its armoured thorax. Holding it up, he scrutinised it from a distance of centimetres. As he had hoped, it hadn't been dead long: the compound eyes still held the breath-taking range of colours that would so tragically mute and fade in just a few hours' time. Somehow the myriad of tiny lenses on the eye's surface created an illusion of infinite depth. Peering in he observed the gently shifting colours and knew that in sunlight the sight was even more striking. He turned his attention to the wings; they were remarkably rigid thanks to the structure of seemingly irregular struts and spars that formed a network like veins in a leaf.

Looking at the abdomen he frowned slightly; the body was too snubbed to be a common variety of *Aeshna*. The pale blue colour could mean that it was a male of the much rarer species *Libellula depressa*. Later today he would visit the library to find out.

After carefully putting the insect back in the box he stood up and went to the two shelves that ran the length of the side wall. Both were stacked with Perspex containers of various shapes and sizes. With one finger held to his lips he scanned the collection before selecting two – one square-shaped for the glove, one shallower and rectangular for the dragonfly. After placing his two finds in their respective containers and snapping the air-tight lids shut he opened the kitchen blind to the morning sun, turned off the light and went to bed.

Chapter 4
The Hunter

'Hello, love,' his mum called out as she heard the front door open. She poked her head out from the kitchen as he dumped his bag down in the hallway. 'I thought you were getting back earlier.'

'I was meant to,' Andy replied, walking towards her. 'But that murder caused a big delay.' The smile remained on her face and she blinked once. 'On the M40 last night?' he prompted.

She looked a little flustered and said, 'I haven't listened to the news this morning. Are you . . .' She searched for the correct terminology. 'Is it your case?'

'Well, I'm involved on it because it took place in our patrol area.'

'Oh,' she said, trying to sound encouraging. 'That will be . . . good experience for you, won't it?' He nodded as they stepped into the kitchen. 'There's something from your grandpa on the table – it arrived with the post this morning.'

He looked at the long cardboard tube and found it oddly touching that his mum didn't want to ruin his surprise by telling him that it was obviously a poster. Somehow she could make him feel like a young boy without even realising it. Then, despite himself, he picked it up and shook it eagerly. 'I bet it's a poster.'

She just smiled and said, 'Would you like a cup of tea? One of those decaffeinated ones like Dr Roberts advised?'

He sat down heavily at the table and said, 'A cup of Dr Roberts' brew would be great, thanks.'

Turning on the kettle, she said, 'Derek and I are off to the garden centre in a minute, we need some bedding plants.'

'Oh,' he replied, picking with one nail at the carefully applied strip of sellotape holding the lid secure at one end. Eventually he succeeded in bending a corner back, and as he peeled it away the paper surface of the tube was torn off too. Then he dug a nail under the plastic rim, prised the lid out of the tube and placed it on the kitchen table. Inside he could see glossy paper, tightly rolled.

'You must be exhausted – have you not had any sleep since yesterday evening?'

'That's right,' he said, forcing a smile as he teased the poster out. It partly unfurled and a handwritten note fell on to the table. Unrolling the poster, he said, 'He's only gone and found a poster of a police car already.' He couldn't help smiling as pride caused him to flush. Upstairs a toilet did the same.

'Aaah, isn't that nice of him?' his mum replied. 'What does the letter say?'

Andy scanned the shaky writing. 'He asks how you are, tells me congratulations about the job, wants to know if the poster is one of the police cars my motorway traffic division uses.' Footsteps were coming slowly down the stairs so he stopped at the P.S., knowing that part wasn't for reading out.

'So are these long hours going to be a regular thing?' she questioned.

'Probably – it's going to be a big case. They think it's related to a couple of others.'

'Gosh,' she replied, not quite sure what to say next. 'Wasn't last night's storm bad? I had to get up and shut the bedroom window. It flattened the last of the daffodils.'

His stepdad walked into the kitchen, straightening the cuff of his jumper. 'Morning, Andy – you look like you're ready for your bed.'

'He's involved on a big murder case, Derek – one that took place last night. And his grandad's sent him a lovely poster.'

'Right-oh,' he replied, leafing through the assorted bits of paper pinned to the cork notice board. 'Have you got those money-off coupons from *Gardening World*, Pat?'

'Yes – they're in my purse already,' she replied, placing the tea in front of her son. A tiny amount spilt over the rim and ran down the side of the cup.

'Good,' Derek replied, turning round. 'So . . . ' Andy watched him replay the first part of the conversation in his head. Ignoring the poster, he said, 'A big investigation. What's it about then?'

Andy looked down at the tiny puddle of spilt tea and saw the smashed head lying in its dark pool. The flashing blue lights had turned the lumps of matter floating around in it a beautiful silvery colour. Introducing details like that into their safely cushioned world of garden centre tours, visits to DIY stores and strolls in the local park was utterly impossible. Besides, they wouldn't allow information like that in – it would simply be screened out the moment it left his lips.

'Oh – someone was killed by the side of the motorway.' He heard himself adopting his stepdad's manner of speech. 'We're not quite sure why – it's early days yet.'

'Well, good luck with it. Come on, Pat – we'd better go if we're going to make the early lunch special. See you later, Andy.'

His mum paused at his side and gently placed a hand on his shoulder. 'You try and get some sleep, love. I've ironed you some fresh shirts.'

'Thanks – see you later,' Andy said cheerfully as the kitchen door shut.

He picked up his tea and, after removing all evidence of the spillage, slowly climbed the stairs. His bedroom was packed with the paraphernalia of his life-long fascination with cars. The walls were plastered with glossy posters of classic sports models and clinical cross-sections of engines and gearbox mechanisms. Lining most of the shelves and the windowsill was his collection of miniature toy cars – old Matchbox ones sitting alongside new larger-scale replicas complete with opening bonnets and accurate plastic engines.

Carefully he placed the poster on his bedside table and read the letter's P.S. while still standing up. As he expected it talked about his dad and how proud he would have been of Andy. A lump formed in his throat as he read that his father had worked on the early prototypes of Saab's fuel-injection mechanism that most probably formed the basis of the one in his patrol car today. The final sentence was a piece of advice about his new job: 'It's what helped me when I started in the Army over sixty years ago, and it will help you today. "Keep your ears and eyes open and your mouth shut." All the best, Alfred Seer, Captain, Her Majesty's Royal Engineers (Retired).'

Andy rememberd his own final comment to Walker and winced. Physically he felt hollow and washed out, but a small part of his mind was racing around madly like an out-of-control dodgem, touching on all that had happened in the last twelve hours. As usual sleep felt some way off so he drew the curtains shut and sat down before the computer in the corner of his room. As it booted up he stared absent-mindedly into his half-drunk cup of tea.

Once the electronic whirrings had stopped he looked at the screen. The tiny wizard stood waiting for his command, the speech bubble by his pointed hat reading, 'Hello, Andy, last night's full moon won't be repeated for another 29 days. What can I do for you today?' For the thousandth time he told himself he'd have to wipe the annoying figure and his scraps of pagan-related trivia from his computer's set-up. But instead he just clicked the hide button and, with a flourish of his cape, the wizard vanished.

He moved the cursor over to the selection of icons and clicked on 'Joy Rider'. The game's introductory footage took over the screen. The view was from just above and behind the roof of an unmarked police car as it sped through a grim urban landscape, careering round corners in pursuit of a Renault 5 turbo. A shaven-headed youth leaned out from the rear passenger window and hurled a beer can at the pursuing car. It spun through the air towards the windscreen, spraying a trail of white foam behind it. Before it hit he pressed the start button of his chosen pursuit scenario. The footage cut to a police car waiting in a side alley off a main road. A few vehicles went past before a car suddenly shot across the field of vision and a panel lit up on the screen: '73 m.p.h.'. By the time he'd pulled out on to the road the car was barely visible in the far distance. Keeping his finger pressed on the throttle key he quickly moved up through the automatic gears and seconds later was doing 96 m.p.h. and closing on the other car fast. Barely 50 metres ahead it veered into a sharp left-hand turn without warning. He hit the brakes and shadowed the manoeuvre, finding himself on a residential road, pedestrians dotting the pavement. Up ahead a mother with a pram stepped out on to a pelican crossing – directly into the path of the accelerating Renault. Barely adjusting its course it burnt across the black and white markings, clipping the corner of the pram and knocking it from the mother's grip into a 360° spin.

Andy slowed up, his way completely blocked. Thinking quickly, he swerved through a gap in the parked cars and mounted the pavement. He passed the pelican crossing and rejoined the road just before a cluster of pedestrians on the pavement.

Now the joyriders knew they were being followed their driving became erratic, signalling right and turning left, overtaking on blind corners and forcing other cars off the road. Andy kept on in dogged pursuit, reporting in his course by scrolling through a panel of street names and highlighting the one he was on by pressing the 'R' key. He knew that after a few more streets he would have provided his HQ with enough information for them to send in back-up cars. Now barely twenty metres in front of him, the joyriders blasted across a mini-roundabout, jinking round a lorry. Hardly checking his speed, Andy took the roundabout the wrong way, avoiding the lorry and gaining on the other car. He was nearly within ramming distance when it suddenly veered on to a grass verge, clumps of grass kicking up from its rear tyres as it wove between two trees, heading for the entrance to a park. It shot through a space created by a missing concrete bollard – just clearing the narrow gap.

Andy hit the grass and his steering lost its sharpness as he skidded on the treacherous surface. He drifted slightly to the left and, as he tried to take the gap the Renault had shot through, realised at the last second he was slightly out. His car smashed into the bollard on his left and the view in front shattered into a thousand fragments to reveal the words 'GAME OVER'.

Normally that manoeuvre would have been simple. He took it as a sure sign he was now truly knackered. Not bothering to switch off the computer he flopped face first on to his bed, clothes still on. Sleep finally overtook him seconds later.

Chapter 5
The Killer

Each step on the narrow wooden stairs creaked under his bulky frame. The gym was on the top floor of the renovated factory, four storeys above him. As he neared the top of the second flight he could hear someone descending. He reached the landing, turned back on himself and looked up the next set of steps. A slightly built man stood at the top. There followed a moment's hesitation and then, to his satisfaction, the man called down, 'After you, mate,' and beckoned with his hand.

Dave nodded and began climbing the stairs two at a time. Level with the other man, he nodded curtly and said under his breath, 'Cheers, pal.'

'No problem,' the man replied as they passed.

At each end of the sign above the gym's entrance was a painting of a sculpted male figure, contorted in the rictus of a bodybuilding pose. The space between the two figures was filled with the word 'Colossus' painted in a squat, heavy type.

He pushed the spring-loaded door open and stepped into the reception area. The man behind the counter looked up. 'All right, Dave?' he asked.

'Fine, mate – yourself?'

'Yeah, not too bad.'

He scrawled his name in the signing-in book and then stepped through the waist-high swing door into the seating area. A couple of blokes he vaguely recognised sat quietly chatting at a table. As he walked past the gym's parrot it cawed 'Hiya' at him – he ignored it. He passed the clothes shop railing selling an assortment of vests and other gym clothing before finally spotting his training partner sitting in a fat chair facing the wide-screen satellite TV.

'Off your arse, you great ponce!' Dave called over.

His mate looked round, smiled, and raised his massive frame out of the seat. They advanced, each man holding his arms slightly too far out from his sides, as if the size of their muscles didn't allow their limbs to hang straight down. Chests out, they clasped hands for an instant.

'All right, Dave, how are you doing?'

'Good,' he replied. 'Got stuck on a bitch of a delivery yesterday down in Kent, though. Didn't get back till fuck knows when. How's work with you?'

'Yeah, all right. Thought I'd bust my hand at the Shebeen on Saturday.'

'Weren't they shutting that place down?'

'They were, but then the council changed its mind,' Jeff replied, holding up one hand and rubbing his forefinger and thumb together.

Dave tilted his head back in acknowledgement.

'Anyway, these twats kicked off for some reason, right in the foyer. Hadn't even got into the main hall. Big mistake – there were five of us on body searches alone. Gav and Ian on the front doors, stopping them from getting out. We gave them a right battering. This one kid, he was definitely on something, took a wind-up this big to swing at me. Fucking caught his fist in mid-air. I tell you, Arnie would have been proud. Twisted his arm round so his head went down and then hooked him, right under his nose. Went down like a sack of shit. That's when I thought I'd broken a knuckle. Anyway we kicked them all the way down the stairs, back on to the street.'

'Fucking idiots. Rest of the night OK?'

'Oh, yeah. By the way, Gav mentioned there's an all-nighter

CORK CITY
29
LIBRARY

coming up soon. He needs some extra help on the doors, if you're interested?'

'Definitely, I need the cash this month.'

'Right, I'll tell him,' Jeff replied as they shouldered their bags and headed into the main gym area.

Although it was many years since the building had been used for its original purpose, the gym had lost none of its industrial grimness. Men laboured at the rows of work-stations which lined the edges of the hall. They sweated and strained to raise and lower their dead loads, only now they were charged for their effort. Jeff and Dave walked alongside a double rack of free weights that stretched down the centre of the long room, barbells packing it from end to end. The blue paintwork on the heavy iron discs was chipped and completely rubbed off in places. Metal crashed in one corner as a man dropped a laden bar back on to a shoulder-press machine. He held up a hand to acknowledge the two newcomers and then moved the weight's setting up a notch. Between the windows, floor-to-ceiling mirrors reflected their images back at them as they strode heavily to the centre of the room. Club-land music boomed from speakers in the ceiling.

'I hate this shit,' said Dave, flicking his eyes upwards.

'Better than some wanky boy-band,' replied Jeff, flexing his thick neck from side to side.

They staked their claim on a nearby bench by draping their tops over it and then moved into a sequence of warm-up movements. Both wore training vests tucked into swirly-patterned dayglo baggy trousers that clasped tightly round their ankles. Their routine was so well established there was little need for any conversation; after a few minutes they began plucking 10kg weights from a stand and piling them on to each end of a chest press bar. Once enough were loaded on they secured them with the turn-keys.

'Who's first?' asked Jeff.

'You are, pal,' replied Dave.

His mate sat down on the end of the bench and then lay back so his chest was underneath the bar. Dave positioned himself on the step behind him, hands lightly guiding the bar as Jeff lifted it clear of the hooks. As he lowered the weights he gradually sucked in breath until the bar was just above his chest then, as he pushed it slowly and deliberately back up, he exhaled in a steady flow.

Dave watched his training partner's muscles as they moved beneath the surface of his flesh. His eyes fixed on the chest as tension built across it; under the immense load the only thing that appeared to be stopping the sternum from cracking clean open was the thick slabs of muscle. In his mind's eye he imagined how his pectorals must look as he did the exercise, and wondered how they compared to his partner's in terms of definition and mass. Twelve reps and they changed places. Once Dave had completed his first set they added another couple of 10kg discs and carried on in workmanlike silence.

Two weight increases later both men were showing signs of tiring. Their breathing had become heavier and, as Jeff neared the end of his last set of presses, the bar began to waver. From his position on the step above, Dave reached down and curled his hands around it.

'Go on, mate, it's all you – I'm hardly helping,' he whispered urgently down at Jeff's straining face.

His arms slowly straightened.

'One more, mate, come on,' Dave encouraged.

As the bar lowered again Jeff filled his lungs with quick shallow gasps. It paused an inch above his chest and then slowly began to rise. As it did so breath whistled from his pursed lips like gas from a sphincter.

'Go on, go on,' urged Dave, his knuckles showing white with the help he was giving. A grunt exploded from Jeff, sending flecks of spit on to Dave's curled fingers. Together, they guided the bar back on to its hooks. 'Nice one,' said Dave, wiping the white dots from the backs of his hands.

After forty minutes they'd completed three other exercises, stopping between each one to gulp from their bottles of sports drink. By the time they'd finished their routine the gym was filling with the end-of-afternoon rush. Gathering their stuff together, they walked ponderously back to the reception area.

'Two of the protein-boost banana things, please,' Jeff called over to the lad behind the counter as they sat down near the TV.

'That was a good one,' said Dave, sitting back and rubbing the base of his neck with one hand.

'Yup,' Jeff agreed. 'Are you on for Saturday morning?'

'Think so – I've just got to check with old Clarke for any weekend deliveries.'

'So what was yesterday's job?'

'Same old shit – some car components to a distributor's down near Dover. Could I find the place? Could I fuck. That and the traffic – Jesus! I was saying to the wife, next job like that and Clarke will have to pay me by the hour. It took so long yesterday my pay worked out the same as a frigging paper boy's.'

The lad placed two frothy pint glasses on the table between them.

'Cheers, mate,' said Jeff, handing him a fiver.

As they gulped at the thick milk-shake the news came on the TV. Headline story was the killing of the night before. As the newsreader recounted the events a photo of the cordoned-off stretch of motorway appeared behind her with the words 'MOTORWAY MURDERER – CHILD TAKEN' super-imposed over the top.

Jeff watched the screen over the rim of his glass. When she moved on to the next item he said to his friend, 'Did you get stuck in that traffic jam?'

Dave shook his head. 'No, I was home by then. Anyway, coming from Dover, I went round the M25 then up the M1 and came off at junction 19.'

'Lucky,' Jeff replied. 'She said they've only just opened it up now. There's some sick fucker out there – there was a kid taken this time too. I tell you, when they find the bastard, the police should just do a suicide job on him. Leave him dangling in the cells.'

Dave saw those eyes staring up at him from the footwell and his head swam. He had to hold the glass to his mouth while he tried to regain his composure. His mate was staring at him, waiting for a reply. He searched his mind for something to say and, wiping his mouth, blurted, 'Thing is, motorways aren't normal places, are they?'

'You what?' said Jeff.

He'd started now so, cautiously, he continued. 'Well, think about it. No one lives there or belongs there. Everyone's just passing through. You're not even allowed to stop on them. There's no Good Samaritan stuff on motorways. Some poor fucker stranded there needing help? You drive straight past. Because those are the rules. And if you are one of them who breaks down, you should be prepared for being stuck in no-man's-land.'

'What – getting brained by some nutter?' Jeff asked, an incredulous smile playing at the corners of his mouth.

'Exactly, mate. I know it's tough but, like I said, the rules are different on a motorway. And look at your average fuck-wit in a car. Half set off without a clue about their vehicle. I mean, how many people drive around who can't even change a tyre?'

'It's one way of looking at it.'

'Come on, it's true. I know that when you travel you go prepared – same as me. You know your motor, you carry spare parts, extra fuel, a new tyre. If you break down you're not waiting hours for some grease monkey to show up and twiddle a frigging lead or spray WD40 on to your spark plugs – which is what 90% of breakdowns are. You fix it yourself and get on your way, right?'

'Yeah – but we're talking murders here.'

Dave broke into a grin. 'OK, I'm being harsh, but you know me – car drivers make my job shit. Every time I'm stuck in a traffic jam because of some twat's crap driving, it's money out of my pocket.'

'Fair enough,' said Jeff. 'I agree there's far too many pricks allowed to drive cars. Too many pricks full stop. But it's one thing taking on some twat who's cut you up or whatever, and it's another snatching some little girl. And I say beasts like that deserve a swift execution, no questions asked. Which is what'll happen if he ever goes inside. Solitary or no, he'll be got to.'

Dave felt the light-headed onset of fear. 'You never know – it might not be a sex thing.'

'Oh, come off it, mate. There's only one reason a bloke snatches a little girl like that.'

Waves of nausea rose in Dave's throat and he gagged on the last of his drink.

'Yeah,' he murmured, his voice hoarse. 'It makes me sick and all.' His mate nodded in agreement and Dave stood up. Inside his baggy tracksuit bottoms his legs were shivering. 'You heading off now?' he asked.

'No – I'm gonna wait for the sport.'

'OK. I'll give you a bell if I'm not on for Saturday.'

He headed out of the reception and, as he went down the stairs, his jaw tensed up. Again.

Chapter 6
The Searcher

The amplified voice always struck him as particularly inappropriate for such a subdued setting. 'The library will be closing in five minutes. Will you please make your way to the doors. Thank you.' He looked up from the book before him, and across numerous empty tables. The light smattering of other people around the main hall were starting to close books and reach for bags, their activity creating muffled echoes that were quickly absorbed by the domed roof above. The last of the evening sunlight cut through the thick, green glass of the panels, lending the huge room a slightly underwater feel.

Turning back to his book, he traced his finger down the identification chart, looking for the dragonfly specimen he'd found the night before. He stopped at the image of *Ortherum cancellatum*. This was his find, and not, as he had guessed, *Libellula depressa*. He noted the name down in a minute and precise hand, next to some more general notes about the lifecycle of dragonflies and their preferred habitats. His specimen had existed at larval stage for around four years, using a hooked and extendable lower jaw to voraciously attack almost any other creature in the pond – including young fish. Once it had emerged as an adult it had a life span of just a few months. He sadly wondered how long it had survived before a car had hit it.

The voice at his shoulder made him jump. 'Could you be on your way now please, sir?' Keeping his head bowed to avoid eye contact, he nodded. Once the footsteps had softly moved away he stole another glance around. The library attendant had stopped beside a young man who lay slumped across a table, fast asleep. Shaking him gently by the shoulder, the attendant said, 'Come on, mate – you can't spend the night here.' The young man woke with a snort of confusion, hair falling over his face. 'Right, yeah, right,' he said croakily.

Closing the book on *Aquatic Life of the British Isles*, he stood up and pushed the chair back under the table. After returning the book to its exact spot on the shelf, he walked quickly down the wide stone steps to the foyer, clicked through the turnstile and stepped into the twilight outside. The library was located on the edge of the city centre, separated from it by a dual carriageway. From here he had two ways of getting home: the walkway over or the underpass beneath the busy lanes. After a moment's deliberation he chose the underpass. Shoulders hunched and head down, his fast, birdlike walk carried his shadow straight across the maze of graffiti that stretched unbroken from one end of the underpass to the other. Emerging at the other side, he took a right-hand fork in the footpath that led into a section of streets lined with solidly built Edwardian town houses.

This was a wealthier part of the city, spacious homes and leafy streets, conveniently located close to the motorway. He always chose a route that carried him past a rectangular-shaped terrace of houses with a courtyard in the middle. The entire terrace was constructed from the same type of stone – even the pavement surrounding it was made of identical stuff, laid down in thick slabs, surfaces worn smooth.

The joins between the pavement stones were so fine they appeared almost forged together, seamlessly merging with the base of the terrace itself to give the whole block a kind of watertight resilience. He envied the inhabitants within, safely sealed in their shell of stone. The only opportunity of seeing into the inner courtyard was through an iron-fenced archway at one end. Within was a communal area for the residents, tastefully landscaped with benches, shrubs and small flower-beds. On occasions like this, when children were playing inside the courtyard, he would pause at the gate and watch, fascinated by the intricacy of their make-believe games. Shrill cries bounced off the ivy-lined inner walls, racing little forms illuminated by the warm glow from surrounding windows. As usual, after a few minutes an adult would emerge from one of the front doors and begin walking towards the gate. 'Can I help you?' it would ask. As usual he turned away without replying and quickly resumed his walk home.

Sometimes, in the silence of the small hours, he would return to the terrace. Even cold and dark it had lost none of its air of impenetrability. The only noise would be the quiet hiss of the sodium streetlights and on damp nights their harsh glare bathed the smooth pavement slabs in a white light, making their surfaces appear to be coated in a sheen of ice. He would totter along, arms held out slightly from his sides, imagining that his feet might fly out from under him at any moment and the back of his skull crack against the stone's unforgiving surface. Sometimes the lamps seemed to bend lower, as if to scrutinise him better, and once that happened he would always be glad to leave the terrace's protective perimeters and return to the rougher surface of the surrounding roads.

Chapter 7
The Hunter

Like herons they sat motionless on the bank, watching the flow of cars passing by. Both had their sun-visors lowered against the late-afternoon sun and in the shadow behind their eyes were dragged momentarily to the side by different cars' features. The curve of a bonnet, an unusual shade of paint, the flash of blonde hair behind a window – details glimpsed for an instant and then forgotten as the vehicle passed from view. Eyes swivelled back to centre and resumed their idle scanning.

After the night of the killing they'd had a couple of days off, and during that time Walker had picked over Andy's final comment, encouraging his resentment of the fresh-faced youth to fester. Once back on shift he sat tight, waiting for any further remarks – but Andy had kept a polite distance, even in the confines of the patrol car. Walker interpreted this silence as a righteous one, and it both piqued him and made him wary of his temporary partner. He wanted to find out just how principled he might turn out to be. Eventually he broke the silence, saying, as if to himself, 'I wonder what he's after.'

'Mmm?' Andy replied.

Walker turned his eyes slightly upwards to the kestrel, fixed in the sky above the roundabout. The two men watched it in silence for a few seconds.

'He's definitely hunting for something,' said Walker as the bird abruptly dropped thirty feet, as if lowered on a wire. Its wings began to battle gravity once again.

'I don't know. What lives this near roads – rats, snakes?' Andy replied, relieved his senior appeared to be relaxing once again.

The bird suddenly plummeted the remaining distance and disappeared into the thick grass. A couple of seconds later it re-emerged and flew quickly away, talons empty and head hung low as if in embarrassment. Both men grinned.

'So, what made you pick motorway traffic patrol as a special attachment?' Walker casually asked without turning his head – well used as he was to talking at right angles.

Andy turned to answer and found himself looking straight into an ear, noticed bristles sprouting from a waxy crust and looked back out of the windscreen. 'Well, I've always been into cars since I was a kid. I think I got it from my grandpa – he was an engineer in the Army and has always explained that sort of stuff to me.'

'Same for your old man?'

Andy looked uncomfortable and began fiddling with the button for the electric window.

'Well, yeah, he was a car mechanic for Saab. Did a lot of rallying too.'

'Did?' Walker coaxed, mind fully alert.

'A hit-and-run driver murdered him.' Walker noted the choice of words. 'He was just walking home one night.'

'Did they catch the driver?' Sympathy filling his voice.

'Nope. Anyway,' Andy's voice changed tempo, 'once I learned to drive I liked cars even more, so it seemed a good idea to find a job that involved driving.'

'So why not a chauffeur or a lorry driver?'

'Well, you know – the police force is one of those jobs, isn't it? Childhood ambitions and all that. Besides, it's a decent career and you get to break the speed limit without being nicked.'

His attempt at humour immediately prompted an encouraging smile from Walker. Not wanting to hammer home too many questions, he changed tack. 'I know what you mean about it being a good career, plus you get the satisfaction of collaring some really shit people.'

'Yeah,' Andy replied, warming to the conversation. 'That's another reason why I stuck with wanting to join the police; it really annoys me seeing some of the stuff that goes on and not being able to do anything about it.'

Walker pushed the conversation forward. 'God – you'll see some stuff over the years, I can tell you. Driving manoeuvres you wouldn't believe people could try – if that's what you mean.'

'Yeah, but not just dangerous driving. I mean generally too. The way people will break the law and then lie and deny to try and worm their way out.'

Alarm bells rang in Walker's head – the lad sounded like he was on a mission. Just what he needed as a partner in the run-up to his retirement. 'So how long have you got on this attachment?'

'I'm not sure. I'm still talking to the co-ordinators in Personnel, but I've explained that this is what I want as my career. At the moment I'm trying to get them to allow me on the advanced driving course. I'm dying to be allowed to drive one of these – see what's under the bonnet. Did you find the test hard?'

It was Walker's turn to joke. 'Oh, I can't remember – it was so long ago.' Andy smiled in return. 'No, it's quite tough, but pay attention and you'll get through. So are you wanting to skip all the other attachments?'

'Hopefully. What's the point in an attachment with vice or drugs if I just want to join the motorway traffic police?'

'I don't know – you might find it interesting to see how other parts of the force operate. That's the point of the attachment system,' Walker answered.

'Maybe, but I doubt it. How long have you been . . .'

The radio cut him off. 'All units in the vicinity of the M40, M42 interchange at junction 11 please respond.'

Walker lifted the handset from its cradle. 'Driver 1214A3 to base, we're on the roundabout at the A502 turn-off.'

'Roger 1214, proceed to just beyond junction 11, we have a three-vehicle RTA reported. Ambulances en route.'

Walker put the car into first and moved out on to the roundabout. 'Put the sirens on then, Andy,' he said, nodding at the dash. Andy flicked the switch and the siren immediately cut in. The car accelerated across the roundabout and powered down the double-lane slip-road. Other vehicles pulled into the slow lane, out of their way. In seconds they were screaming down the fast lane, everything peeling away beside their vehicle. Andy gripped the edge of the seat with his left hand and fought back the urge to whoop with delight.

Walker, on the other hand, was quietly mulling over their conversation. All he'd wanted to do was chug along nice and easy to his last day. But now he'd been dumped with some eager kid, champing at the bit, thinking he could single-handedly turn the tide of stupid drivers and racing idiots. Well, King fucking Canute, you've got a lesson to learn, he thought. Walker saw a way of injecting a bit of interest into the drag of his final weeks: he'd see if, in the time remaining, he could shatter the upstart's enthusiasm. Get him to think twice about his ambition of being a motorway traffic policeman. Now both of them were smiling inwardly.

Within a few minutes they passed a sign for junction 11, and a few hundred metres on, the multiple red bursts of brake lights being applied told them they were nearing the accident scene. The overhead information system was already flashing '20 MPH' at the cars passing beneath it. Walker cut across on to the hard shoulder and their patrol car cruised past the back of the three-lane queue.

'Right,' he said, flicking off the siren, 'it looks like we're the first here, so we secure the accident scene, check for any serious injuries and then think about clearing the lanes.'

Up ahead they could see figures huddled on the grass verge. One person was slumped in a sitting position, being comforted by another. Walker brought the patrol car to a stop and they both climbed out. In the distance they could hear other sirens approaching. Two cars lay skewed across the slow and middle lanes, one with its front end heavily stoved in. An ugly smear of black rubber and a spray of glass across the road revealed where the collision had taken place. Other vehicles were fighting to get into the fast lane so they could edge round the crashed cars and continue on their way.

'OK? Everyone all right?' Walker said loudly, approaching the huddle of people. Various heads nodded.

'Where's the third vehicle?' Andy asked him as they neared the group. Several people overheard him and pointed off to the left at the field below the raised motorway lanes. A twenty-foot gouge ended at a car. It lay on its roof, wheels pointing at the sky, tarnished undercarriage exposed to the sun. Like a cigarette stubbed out in a plate of food, it looked horribly out of place jammed there amongst the lush green shoots.

'Anyone still inside?' Walker asked sharply.

'No, she's here,' said a girl comforting the woman sprawled on the grass verge. Andy squatted down in front of her; there were no obvious injuries. Only her messed-up hair, glazed look and muddy shoes gave any indication of her ordeal. 'She's in shock – is there a blanket in your patrol car?' the girl asked.

'Yeah, hang on.' He quickly retrieved it. The traffic now stretched back a good four hundred metres.

'Andy, get the bollards out,' Walker instructed him. 'You need to close off the inside lane. Start about one hundred metres back. Direct the cars across into the middle lane and line up the bollards on a diagonal, stretching back to here. I'll take statements and clear the accident site.'

'OK,' he replied, handing the blanket to the girl and removing the stack of bollards from the boot of the car. Then he jogged a hundred metres back up the hard shoulder as two more patrol cars and an ambulance approached. Hurriedly he placed a bollard on the white line at its edge. Next he walked in between the stationary cars to the fast lane which was still crawling forward inch by inch. He signalled the approaching car to stop and then began waving the cars from the middle and slow lanes across into the fast lane. Before the gap he created was filled he placed a couple of bollards in the road. The drivers whose way he'd just barred realised they were now trapped and began immediately looking behind them to try and cross into the moving lane.

As the ambulance and patrol cars passed the last one slowed down and an officer jumped out. 'Here you go, mate, I'll give you a hand.'

Between them they quickly cleared the inside lane, placing bollards behind them as they went. By the time they had worked their way back to the scene of the crash a tow truck was already there, hauling off the crumpled car. Other officers were sweeping broken glass and fragments of bumper off the road. 'Cheers,' said Andy as he placed the last of the bollards down.

'No problem,' replied the officer, striding away towards the ambulance.

Walker appeared at Andy's side. 'Come on! Come on!' He began waving on the cars that had made it into the fast lane and were now slowing down to stare at the crash. Walker looked at Andy. 'Fucking rubber-neckers: make the delay far worse.'

They both turned and glanced back up the motorway – the blue sky was reflected back at them by a river of shimmering wind-screens. 'This, my friend, is what most of the job is really about.' Walker continued sweeping his arms across his body. 'Car chases and all that glamorous stuff it isn't. You'll soon sympathise with the staff in NCP car parks.'

Andy stood lamely next to him, feeling as though he should be doing something too. He began to wave his arms. 'Keep moving, keep moving,' he told the cars as they crept slowly by.

Chapter 8
The Killer

The radio quietly droned as Sally placed the last of the bowls on the draining board and said, 'OK, Dave, you wipe her face and strap her into the car seat while I get the swimming stuff ready.'

He looked over the top of his Sunday paper. His daughter slumped sideways in the high-chair watching her mother, one leg absentmindedly kicking backwards and forwards. She seemed totally unconcerned by the explosion of breakfast cereal surrounding her mouth and stretching in flecks right up to her forehead.

In the background the news announcer repeated the appeal the entire country was now familiar with. 'The buckle on Laura's shoe is very distinctive. It's made from a silver-coloured metal, shaped like a daisy. The leather of the shoe is bright red and on the inside are the words "First Steps, Size 9". If anyone finds a shoe fitting this description they are urged to contact the police immediately.'

'I don't think they're ever going to find that little girl. Not alive at least,' his wife suddenly said. He shot a glance at her. She was leaning next to the sink, smoothing moisturiser into her hands. 'It's awful. Every time I see the mother on TV making another appeal I think how you and me would cope if anything ever happened to our Jasmine. Can you imagine it? God, it terrifies me.'

With a massive effort he looked into her eyes. Once she had

registered the intensity that burned in his, he knew no answer was necessary. He folded up the paper. 'Right, you little monster – swim time!'

Sally watched as he took the wet flannel from the sink by her side and gently began wiping the remnants of food from the baby's face and hands. As she stood there a warmth ran through her as if blown on a breeze. Pausing to run a hand across his shoulders, she kissed the back of his head.

As soon as Jasmine was clean he lobbed the flannel and her bib into the sink and lifted her clear of the seat. Once in the air she began kicking her legs in excitement and he felt the muscles in her tiny torso flexing beneath his palms. The sensation brought memories from the motorway flashing back and he had to fight the urge to snatch his arms away and drop his daughter to the floor. Holding her at arm's length and avoiding her eyes, he lowered her into the car seat and by the time he'd clicked the straps together his wife was waiting by the door with the sports bag. He picked up the car seat and they stepped out on to the street. His car – an immaculately clean silver Ford Escort (16-valve) – was parked in its spot immediately in front of the house, with a generous gap on each side of it. His neighbours knew better than to box him in. He pulled out on to the road and stopped. 'Do the bollard then,' he said.

With a sigh, his wife climbed out, opened the boot, removed the 'No Parking' bollard and placed it in the gap he'd just created. She climbed back in and they set off to the main road at the end of their street. Traffic flowed past both ways in a steady stream. He needed to turn right. He wound his window down to make sure other drivers could clearly see his face then, as soon as a slight gap appeared in the traffic to his right, edged his car on to the road, staring at the driver of the oncoming car. It had to let him out. Looking to his left he did the same thing and was able to make the right turn. As he pulled away he gave a quick nod to the drivers he'd forced to stop. Fifty metres up the road the traffic ground to a halt behind a bus as it picked up a load of passengers. He began tapping his left forefinger impatiently on the top of the gear stick. The traffic edged forward again, eventually reaching the T-junction at the end of the road where it stopped once more as the lights turned to red. The flow of cars was solid on the main road they were waiting to join too.

'The pool attendant said last week that Jasmine's really good in the water. Said she's a natural.'

'Yeah?' he replied, counting the cars separating him from the lights. Nine including the bus. He'd only make it through when it next turned green if the bus set off at a decent speed and none of the cars in front pissed around for too long trying to find first gear. The lights changed and, sure enough, the driver three cars ahead took a couple of seconds to release his handbrake and put it in first. Dave's heart began beating faster. 'Come on, you fucking idiot,' he cursed under his breath. They crawled forward, his eyes flitting from the traffic lights to the car in front and back again. Three cars separating him from the lights . . . and they changed to orange. Instead of accelerating through, the car in front kept its speed steady so as Dave reached them, the lights were on red. 'Shit!'

'They're starting a class next month for Mums and Tots; I think Jasmine will love it. You know, being with other kiddies, learning,' his wife said from the back.

'Nice one,' he said, watching the traffic on the main road going through the lights ahead like a hawk. His turned orange and there were still cars trying to squeeze through the junction. The instant he saw green he pulled out and, because the last two cars were caught halfway across, they barred his right turn. He moved his car so its front bumper was practically touching the side of an elderly couple's car in front and hit the horn. The trapped driver looked uneasily at him and held two palms up at the cars in front.

Immediately Dave shoved his shaved head out of the window. 'If you hadn't gone through on fucking orange you wouldn't be sat there like a cunt now!' The old woman looked across at him with fear in her eyes. She said something to the man and he began to close his window. 'Yeah, wind it up, you prick, you've fucking wound me up already!' Dave shouted as the traffic began moving forward again.

His wife had sunk down in the back seat and was seemingly

engrossed in shaking a rattle in front of the baby's face. 'God, I could rip the throat out of twats like him,' he cursed.

'Come on, Dave – it's only a Sunday,' she said tensely.

'It's only a Sunday,' he mimicked. 'Tell that to the arseholes out there!'

They crept slowly onwards, closed in on all sides by cars that were either parked or moving at less than walking pace.

'Put the radio on, hon,' his wife asked.

He flicked it on and a patient voice filled the interior of the car.

'There's still one lane of the westbound M62 blocked by an accident at junction 23 near Huddersfield. Tim says the queue now stretches back a couple of miles. If you're heading north towards the roadworks on the M6 in Cheshire at junction 18, Holmes Chapel, the back of the queue is now at junction 15. George says there's also a broken-down car blocking one lane of the motorway outside Sandbach services. The northbound M42 in Leicestershire remains closed after an accident between junctions 10 and 11, Tamworth and the A444. Bobby says traffic in the area is horrendous. Lesley says there's an overturned car causing some problems on the southbound A24 by Horsham. Yaggi reports an accident on the A1 in Cambridgeshire, expect some severe delays heading towards Stamford, and on the A12 in Essex an accident is causing southbound delays between Whitfield and Hadfield-Peverel. In Kent an accident is blocking the westbound M20 between junctions 2 and 3, and please take extra care on the A39 in north Devon as a car is in the hedge on the nasty bend near the Clovelly turning. Emergency service vehicles are parked across the road . . .'

He let out a long, shivering sigh of disgust and punched the retune button with one knuckle. The radio settled on 'Roll FM – hits from when music was for listening to'. A Marillion song was playing and he began tapping his forefingers in appreciation. The traffic thinned out a fraction. His attention turned to the week ahead. A few local drop-offs Monday and Tuesday then a Thursday-morning delivery to Southampton where he was picking up some electrical components and taking them on to Bristol. It was less than two weeks since his last bit of sport, and he wasn't sure if he was in the mood for some more. See how the traffic going down to Southampton is, he thought. Next thing his foot was jamming on the brakes as his mind registered the figure in the periphery of his vision.

'Bloody hell,' his wife said as she banged into the back of his seat. He'd been completely oblivious to the pelican crossing ahead – as they lurched to a stop his front bumper was over the black and white stripes. The young woman in front fixed him for a second longer with a hostile look and then stepped warily forward, suddenly revealing the little girl she'd been shielding. The youngster didn't take her frightened eyes off him quite so fast and, as their glances met, the image of those other eyes he tried so hard to forget stared him in the face once more. He winced and his own eyes shut as if sand had been thrown into them, but still the unblinking gaze of the child filled his vision.

'I think it's clear now, Dave,' his wife said sarcastically from behind.

'Yeah, yeah,' he answered, armpits prickling as his sweat pores opened up. He focused on the cars in front, molars clamped together, studying the registrations and working out how old each vehicle was.

The sharp smell of chlorine always seemed stronger to him in the foyer than in the pool itself. 'See you in there then,' his wife called out as she pushed through the female changing-room doors. He didn't know what it was about pools that unsettled him – perhaps it was the slippery-looking floors and over-excited kids running around inside. Whatever, it only made his headache worse.

Once in a cubicle he sat down and took some deep breaths. His jaw ached and he massaged the point below each ear with his thumbs. After dumping his stuff in a locker and struggling with the catch on the wristband, he walked gingerly towards the foot-bath, aware of people's double glances as they noticed his unnatural size. Stepping into the shallow trough, he made a conscious effort not to flinch at the coldness of the water. Into the main pool and the whoops and screams of children suddenly grew louder. Keeping his eyes away from their little figures, he stepped carefully round to the smaller pool where his wife sat, daughter cradled in her arms.

'You OK, darling?' she asked as he sat in the water beside her.

'Yeah, just a bit of a headache. Jesus – I didn't know they could make arm-bands that small. Come on then, let's see her swim.'

Cupping the back of the infant's head and hips Sal lowered the tiny body into the water and then extended her arms. 'Kick, kick, kick, kick, kick!' she said in a sing-song voice. The infant lay rigid in the water, eyes staring upwards, trying to make sense of the strange new medium distorting her mother's voice. She flexed her fingers and spasmodically kicked one leg. 'Good girl!' said her mother.

Dave smiled. 'Go, Jas – use your legs.' He reached out a hand to grip her feet gently then changed his mind about touching her, leaving his hand outstretched below the water. She risked looking around, but apart from that her face remained tense, lips pursed firmly shut. After ten minutes or so they climbed out and sat on the heated seats at the pool's edge.

As Sal gently towelled the baby dry, she said, 'After those classes I mentioned, she won't need any arm-bands.'

Dave sighed heavily. 'Sal, they sound like a good idea but we're fucked for money. I've got the bastard road-tax and car insurance burning a hole in the kitchen shelf. We can't afford stuff like that for her.'

'Dave, calm down. It's free. It's one of those council-run educational courses that costs nothing if you're on the Social.'

'Is it?' he asked with relief. 'Nice one.' He stared out across the main pool for a few seconds. 'Right, have you got my shower gel?'

'In the changing bag.'

'OK, see you in the café.' He walked slowly back round to the men's showers, but each one was taken. He stood, arms crossed, waiting for someone to leave. A young kid stared wide-eyed at the size of him. 'Come on, Luke – share with me,' his dad said and the boy immediately went to him. Dave nodded to the father and stepped under the hot spray.

He'd eaten a Mars Bar and half a packet of crisps by the time Sally pushed Jasmine into the café area.

'Ooh – give us some of them,' she said, her damp hair held back in a bright orange hairband. 'I'm always starving after a swim.'

She hung her handbag on the back of the buggy and whipped the packet from his hands, shoving a handful into her mouth. 'Mmmm, lovely!' she mumbled, as a couple of fragments fell from her lips.

'Animal,' Dave replied, smiling as she poured the last pieces directly into her mouth. Looking into the buggy, he saw his daughter was already asleep. They walked to the double exit doors and he pulled one open. As Sally pushed the buggy through he glanced down at his trainer. 'Lace undone,' he said, crouching down, his shoulder propping the door open.

Sally stepped out on to the red-brick causeway leading up to the pool's entrance and picked a dandelion from amongst the litter in the raised flowerbed. From away to her side the sound of roller-blades quickly approached. She was leaning over the buggy, threading the flower into Jasmine's harness, when the first skater appeared, hooded top over his head. He hooked one hand into the crook of Sally's elbow, and, using his momentum, yanked her sharply round so she fell backwards. She squeaked in surprise and pain as Dave looked up from inside the foyer.

The second hooded skater shot into view, jumped to a double-footed stop and snatched her handbag from the back of the buggy. Dave launched himself out of the doorway, grabbed the back of his neck and started to squeeze. The skater let out an agonised cry and the handbag dropped to the ground. Dave's other hand clamped him under his armpit and the lad was hurled face first into the twisted gorse bush in the centre of the flowerbed. The other skater made to step around Sally but Dave blocked his way. Quickly he pivoted on his rollerblades and moved towards the flight of steps leading up from the car park. As he started to bump down them, the heel of Dave's hand hit him squarely between the shoulder blades. His skates prevented him from getting any sort of grip and he flew down the first half-dozen before overbalancing and tumbling down the remainder. He lay perfectly still at the bottom.

'Are you OK?' said Dave, helping Sally to her feet.

'I think so,' she replied, rubbing her upper arm. 'It happened so 'quickly.' Anxiously she peered into the buggy, but Jasmine had slept through everything. Dave was eyeing the bag snatcher as he tried to extricate himself from the thorn-covered branches.

'Let's go back inside and call the police,' said Sally.

'No way. No police, we're off. Come on.' He picked up the entire buggy and carried it down the flight of steps. Sally followed him.

'Is he all right?' she asked, looking at the motionless figure.

'He'll be playing dead if he fucking knows what's good for him,' replied Dave, putting the buggy down and holding out a hand to Sally. She took it gratefully.

'Shouldn't you check him?' she asked.

'OK – you head for the car. We're over there,' he said, nodding towards the right-hand side of the car park. Shakily she started off with the buggy. Dave let her take a few steps, then bent over the figure curled amongst the empty crisp packets. 'Not dead, are you, pal?' he whispered. The figure moaned. 'That's good. Well, I'll be seeing you then.' Casually he swung his foot at the back of the lad's head, and then caught up with his wife. 'He was all right, a few grazes, that's all.'

Once in the car Sally said, 'The little shits. If I'd had hold of the buggy, the whole thing would have gone over. Bastards!'

'Well, it all went fucking pear-shaped for them,' replied Dave, starting the engine.

'You were brilliant,' she said, leaning over from the back seat and rubbing his shoulders. 'They never knew what hit them!' She laughed a breathless, adrenaline-filled laugh. 'That first one – you must have thrown him twelve foot!' She squeezed his biceps, and years of weights were suddenly worth it.

'Took on the wrong fucking family, didn't they?' he said, swelling with pride.

Sally laughed. 'Took on the wrong father, more like it. Our bodyguard!'

Dave hadn't felt so good in ages. He reached back and squeezed her hand as they accelerated across the car park. But instead of roaring away up an empty road, a slowly moving procession of cars greeted them. They eased into it, suddenly anonymous, just part of the flow. Gradually their breathing slowed down as they edged along, until the car rolled to a stop. He sighed deeply. 'What's causing that now?' he asked as much to himself as to Sally, winding his window down and looking through the gap between the vehicles in front. Halfway up the street a cab was attempting a three-point turn but, because the traffic was so tight to either side, it was having to shuttle back and forth across the road. 'Bastard cabbies – they're well out of order.' His heart began to beat faster.

On the pavement beside him people strolled slowly past. Eventually they moved off again, making their tortuous way home. A few minutes later they joined the huge queue for the traffic lights at the T-junction he'd turned out of earlier. 'Where does everyone go on a Sunday?' he suddenly said. 'It's like bloody rush hour every frigging day.'

His wife didn't bother answering as they edged forward, stopped, edged forward, stopped. He sat with one elbow hanging out of the car window and in his side mirror watched a moped wend its way up the gap between the two lanes. On impulse he edged the car into the middle of the road. 'Fit through that, smart-arse,' he whispered under his breath. The moped reached his car and stopped. He watched with satisfaction out of the corner of his eye as the helmet bobbed from side to side, the rider trying to work out distances.

Abruptly it steered round the back of his car and overtook him on the inside. Once in front it slowed down, and with his right hand extended the rider raised a gloved middle finger at Dave. 'Bastard!' he bellowed, reaching for the seat-belt release and stalling the engine. But the moped was off, dodging its way through the traffic once more. Dave's heart pounded in his chest. Someone's going to pay for that, he thought, as his daughter's cries filled the car.

Chapter 9
The Searcher

Walking back from the shop, bag of bread and tins dangling from one thin arm, he turned off his usual route and headed towards the big roundabout. He hadn't foraged for a while now and the urge to do so was becoming irresistible. This detour was a way of dampening the urge, if only for a few hours before darkness fell. Being part of a road extension scheme to give access to a new housing development on some old floodplain, the roundabout hadn't been there long. The 24-hour garage directly on the other side was the perfect excuse for walking across it. As he moved through the ankle-length blades, hazy memories of standing in grass of a similar length returned. Waiting in the rain as his two cousins dripped abuse at him from under the bus shelter's corrugated roof. Cursing him for making them share a bedroom, for ruining their holidays. When would the social workers return to take him away? they would ask. Popular at their school, they had no problem getting the rest of their classmates to join in too: as the New Boy he was a natural victim.

He kept his head lowered, all the while furiously scanning the ground at his feet for any interesting items. He knew it was a poor imitation of what the central reservation itself had to offer – mainly just litter blown there by the wind and the odd empty cigarette lighter tossed from a car – but it was still worth the odd visit. He knew he had to look carefully; there could be no pausing to examine something merely glimpsed. And there was certainly no actual stopping to pick anything up, because he knew the man in the garage was watching. He could feel the prod of his stare from over fifty metres away.

But today the worst thing possible had happened – the council had been and cleared up the litter. The grass was shorn and sterile, plucked clean of all debris. He reached the other side without having seen a single item. Crestfallen, he stopped to buy some sweets from the garage to justify his detour and then trudged home.

That decided it then – he would forage tonight. Letting himself back into his house, he sat down on his hard kitchen chair and waited for the day to end. He already knew which section of motorway he was heading for. About one and a half hours away, he'd spotted it on a scouting trip a couple of weeks earlier. The central reservation was ideal: wide and bumpy, flanked to each side with crash barriers, and with good parking on a dirt track just one field away. Once the light in his kitchen was so dim he couldn't read the dates on the calendar hanging on the wall, he rose to his feet, removed some crisp new shopping bags from the second drawer down and set off.

Loose stones made a rubbery popping noise as he rolled to a stop. There was no light visible except a dull glow on the horizon from a nearby town. With practised ease he climbed into his army overalls and applied the camouflage cream to his face and hands. Once he'd locked the car he climbed over the wooden fence and made his way carefully across the lumpy field. A low droning told him the motorway was just beyond. As he got to the other side of the field he dropped on to all fours and crawled to the wire fence. The grey tarmac lay just twenty metres away, down a shallow grassy slope. Even though the traffic was light he waited over half an hour before it was completely clear in both directions. Then he raced across to his haven, throwing himself flat on his face, breathing in the fibrous smell of the grass, gratefully clenching handfuls of it.

It was an average search; by the time the grass ran out and was replaced by a barren concrete stretch he'd collected four worthwhile items in as many hours. Turning round, he burrowed his way back towards his starting point. By now the traffic had thinned to almost nothing and he was quickly able to cross back to the empty field. But he'd misjudged the exact point where he'd first crossed by around seventy metres, and so found himself at the edge of the field by a narrow strip of trees. As he made his way along the edge a faint mewing noise caught his attention. He paused mid-step, one foot hanging in the air, eyes staring unfocused ahead as he pinpointed the direction of the sound. It was coming from amongst the trees to his right. Noiselessly he stepped between them, quickly noticing a couple of large holes in the bare earth by the trunks. From right in front of one of the entrances the sound was repeated. Stepping forward again, a twig snapped under his foot and he grimaced at the sound. But to his surprise it only made the plaintive cries more persistent. Leaning down, he finally spotted it. Half-blind and barely able to stand trembled the tiny form of a baby fox. Immediately his mind connected the flattened adult he'd seen on the cruel lanes earlier with this starving little creature. He extended a hand to its face and it started trying to suckle on one of his fingers. He picked it up and tucked it inside his overalls against his chest; it felt cold and started nuzzling towards his armpit. He cupped the shivering body, charmed by its unknowing innocence. As he stepped through the grass he reshaped the mould of his mouth and cooed soothing sounds down the front of his overalls.

Back at the car he opened the boot and placed the cub in a cardboard box, which he then put on the floor in front of the passenger seat. He started the engine and turned the heater to warm. Quickly he went through his after-forage routine, transferring the finds from his pockets into shopping bags and lining them up on the back seat. On the motorway he stopped at the first set of services he reached and silently purchased some milk from the attendant imprisoned in the petrol station kiosk. Though unused to feeding from anything other than its mother's teat, the cub managed to lap the milk up thirstily from the palm of his hand.

He sat back and examined the fragile form in his lap. It looked at him with jaws slightly open, tongue protruding and tiny globules of milk stuck like minuscule Christmas baubles on the spikes of hair around its mouth. Chestnut eyes, shining with the inner light of survival, regarded him almost lustfully – knowing that it had found another source of food. It flicked its tongue across its whiskers and continued its shallow panting. He found its helplessness, its total reliance on him, delicious – it filled him with a sensation of power. He placed his hand behind its head and pressed his fingers through the pelt. Feeling beneath the fur he realised that its neck was no thicker than a chicken's. And he wondered if, like a chicken, it would appear half its size once stripped of its covering.

An hour later he gently placed the box on the doorstep and straightened up. Apart from the animal's quick breaths, all was dark and quiet. He reached towards the door handle, raising his hand past it to the doorbell. As it sounded he turned away and walked swiftly down the short driveway. At the gateposts he paused and looked back at the house. The porch light had already come on, bathing the box in its glow. As he moved off, his shadow momentarily passed over the brass plaque that read 'M. Endacott M.R.C.V.S. Veterinary Surgeon'.

Chapter 10
The Hunter

'Ah, Ray – little errand before you go out on patrol.' The duty officer was holding up a piece of fax paper.

The pair walked over to the desk and Walker took the sheet from the desk-bound man. The instructions were printed in the dot-matrix of the fax machine and across the top a blue biro note had been added which read, 'Walker / Seer to check start of their 1–10 p.m. shift, Tuesday.'

'A kind request from no less than Scotland Yard. Allocated to your good selves.'

'Why, thank you very much,' replied Walker with over-elaborate politeness.

The message was sending them out to a distributor of car electrical components on the edge of the city. One of the employees had been an RAC driver until just over a year before. It was their job to compare his shift rotas with the dates of the three killings.

'The bloke in charge of all the drivers knows you're coming; just ask for Mr Clarke at the security gate.'

They pulled up at the barrier and the guard slid back his glass window.

'Afternoon, officer.'

'Afternoon, we're here to see a Mr Clarke. He's expecting us.'

'Oh, yes, he phoned through already. Just head round to the left and follow the signs for "Depot". Mr Clarke's office is at the end of the corridor on the right-hand side of the bay area.'

The barrier swung up and they followed the road round. The rear of the building was open-ended with a series of eight numbered bays. Lorries were backed into a few of them, allowing trolleys and boxes to be loaded on. They walked to the right side of the dock and into a narrow partition-walled corridor with abrasive carpet tiles covering the floor. In the room at the end a balding man stood up and opened the door.

'Hello, officers. Come in, please.'

They walked down the corridor, stepped into the room and he shut the door behind them.

'Mr Clarke? Sergeant Walker and Constable Seer. I believe you've been told that we need to check some shift rotas for one of your drivers.'

'Yes. Cup of tea before we get started?'

'Thanks, white with three sugars,' replied Walker.

Clarke looked at Seer. 'White with none, thanks.'

'Please, sit down,' said Clarke, pressing the buttons on a tiny vending machine in the corner. It spewed out a stream of brackish water into white plastic cups. 'OK. So you need the last four months' shift rotas for a Mr Gregory.'

'That's right,' answered Walker.

'Well, here they are.' He opened a grey file and examined the top sheet. 'This folder actually goes right back to the start of the tax year, but each week's shifts are clearly marked. He's been with us almost fourteen months. Satisfactory reference from the RAC, his previous employer. Can I ask what it's in connection with?'

Walker replied, 'It's just routine enquiries, sir. There's no reason for you to worry.'

'Fine,' said Clarke, standing up and handing over the file. As the two officers leant forward to examine the top sheet, Clarke saw a figure looming at the glass behind them. Andy noticed the movement and looked round, directly at the man captured in the doorframe. While the officer's head was turned Clarke widened his eyes in warning and glanced to his left. The figure hesitated, met Andy's inquisitive glance for a second, then backed away to the despatches office at the top of the corridor.

'Well, if I can leave you two with it, I've just got to help with a delivery.'

'You go ahead, we'll only be a few minutes,' replied Walker as he flipped the top sheet over. Andy turned back to the file and Clarke hurried from the room.

After quarter of an hour they had checked off all the times and destinations of Gregory's deliveries on the nights of the killings. Walker could see immediately that the man was nowhere near two of the murders. He closed the file and they left the office, teas untouched behind them. As they emerged into the loading bay they saw Clarke pacing around. When he spotted them he walked over.

'Thanks very much for your assistance,' said Walker. 'The file's on your desk.'

'No problem, hope everything's fine?'

'Absolutely,' replied Walker as they walked out.

Chapter 11
The Killer

'It's just a swift one, Dave, if you're up for it. A bunch of boxes to the distribution warehouse on the Mill Estate.'

Dave looked at his watch; he was due to meet Jeff in one hour forty. 'Tell you what, I'll do it if there's some cash waiting for me when I get there – you owe me for my last five trips.'

'Last five? Sorry, mate, I've got well behind. Yeah, that's no problem, see you in a quarter of an hour?'

'Yup.' Dave put the phone down and grabbed his van keys. He jogged straight to the lock-up, unclasped the padlock and heaved the folding door up into the roof. Light from the grey sky shone into the front of the garage, catching on the edge of the tiny sink just inside the door and illuminating the concrete floor just enough for him to negotiate his way between the rubbish strewn all over it and get to the driver's door. However the dirty wash of light fell short of his mother's old wardrobe wedged into the garage's dark end. It brooded there silently, doors firmly shut. Then, just as he was about to unlock the van, a muffled scratching noise sounded from the far end of the garage. He froze rigid, staring at the wardrobe's dark outline. A second later there was a fluttering noise immediately followed by a chorus of high-pitched peeps. He realised it was a bird's nest, probably under the roof's overhang behind the wardrobe. His shoulders visibly relaxed and he inserted the key into the van door.

'*In West Lothian an accident is blocking the northbound A899 between the Houston interchange and M8 at junction 3, Livingstone. The accident and roadworks on the northbound M6 in Cheshire have combined to create a queue something like six miles long back to junction 14. Two problems southbound on the M1. Firstly there's a very long queue approaching a car crash at junction 30, Bob says he's just joined it at junction 35. Once you're through that there is plenty of heavy congestion leading to the roadworks at junction 28, Alfreton. The accident on the A1 at Darlington has now been cleared, but police report a queue of some three miles in both directions which will take some time to disperse . . .*'

At the depot he quickly parked up, not noticing the patrol car tucked in by the side of the wheelie bins, and went straight to the corridor leading to Clarke's office. As he got to the door he could see two men sitting with their backs to him – one with a skinny neck craning to see whatever the fat older one had on the desk. Clarke was just standing up. As he spotted him he widened his eyes in warning, then looked to the doorway of the despatches office in the corridor behind him. Dave stood still and glanced again at the two figures – meeting the younger one's eyes and seeing the jackets that marked them as police. He quickly backed up the corridor, through a doorway, and stood there, head hanging down, wondering whether to bolt back out into the loading bay and make a run for it. He heard Clarke's door open and a single set of footsteps come down the short corridor. Through his panic a glimmer of relief also flickered; it looked like this was finally an end to his sport. Then Clarke stepped into the room.

'Fucking hell, Dave, that was close. I've got the rozzers in there sniffing over one of my salaried driver's records. Last thing I needed was you bursting in and asking for cash – you don't even officially exist in this place. Jesus, I could see it all going pear-shaped! Fucking tax inspectors and all that.' He shook his head in relief. 'Right, these are the boxes. I'll give you a hand getting them to your van. We need you out of here, top speed.' Dave's emotions were all over the place, so he just kept quiet as Clarke piled up the boxes on his forearms. 'Right, quick – back out the door,' he said as they hurried round the side.

At the van Dave had finally got his wits together enough to ask, 'So have you got my cash?'

Clarke looked at him in disbelief. 'No. No, I haven't. Because it's currently in an envelope sat under the twitching snout of a Sergeant bloody Porker. Now fuck off, Dave – it'll be here for you next delivery.'

Bastard, he thought, and stomped round to the driver's door, slamming it shut behind him. Once through the security gate he pushed his way into the long line of slowly moving cars and looked at his watch. Just over an hour to meeting Jeff. It would be close, he thought. He reached the top of a rise in the road and saw the queue of traffic ahead, a patchwork of different-coloured roofs interspersed with the odd van and lorry.

'*Big Dave reports a car fire on the M4 westbound between 4B and 5. It's on the hard shoulder but smoke is slowing traffic down to a crawl. In the Highlands the A82 is closed to lorries and buses after an accident at Glencoe; some cars are getting through. The M5 getting on to the M6 is, according to Janet, absolutely stacked. The M42 is still shut at junction 8 and won't open again until tomorrow morning. On the A11 there's been an accident by the racetrack at Snetterton, traffic is extremely congested in both directions while police try to instigate a contraflow system. Thanks for the calls from the M62 in West Yorkshire where two westbound lanes are blocked by a jack-knifed car and caravan at . . .*'

Fuck it, he thought, palms slapping against the steering wheel as he executed a quick three-point turn. Some wanker beeped him as he headed for the ring road but soon he was on the dual carriageway that curled round the outer edge of the city, roaring to within inches of other cars and flashing his lights until they got out of his way. But after a few minutes his way became completely clogged again. A slower car overtaking a coach overtaking a caravan had created a bottleneck of vehicles. Eventually the car cleared the coach and pulled into the middle lane. Once it was his turn to overtake Dave tried to catch the car driver's eye, disgust twisting his lips. Once clear he moved into the middle lane and sat with right arm raised, raking the inside of his nose. He became aware of a sports car overtaking him, and as he glanced to his side to check it wasn't a woman driving, the female in the passenger seat – almost touching distance away – hurriedly turned to look straight ahead. He smiled to himself, concluding, as he wiped the snot down the side of his seat, that she'd been checking out his arm muscles. You can buy flash motors, baby, but you can't buy this physique, he thought, ramming his finger back up his nose.

As his exit approached he passed a big roadworks sign telling him that his lane would terminate in 400 yards. He watched with satisfaction as all the traffic in front began to melt into the inner lane. That cleared the way for him and he shot up the empty stretch of road, past the queue on his left, ignoring the subsequent signs telling him that his lane would close in 200, 100, 50 yards. Right at the barrier itself he finally signalled left and forced his way in. To his surprise the scrawny-necked geek in the car he'd cut in front of briefly beeped him. A tentative reprimand. Dave stamped on the brakes, leapt from the van, and to the driver's obvious dismay marched up to his car. He brought his snarling face to within millimetres of the windscreen. 'Do you fucking want some, you little prick!' he shouted. 'Well, do you?' The young man just sat there, ashen-faced. Dave straightened up, took a long deliberate snort and gobbed on to the windscreen in front of him. Then he turned around and strode back to his van, relishing his moment of triumph.

He set off across the roundabout, and once back on the busier city streets started using the van's horn as an auditory club, battering the back of obstructing vehicles, brandishing it threateningly at pedestrians who looked like they might venture into his path. So when some blonde in a little Micra nipped out of a side street, causing him to brake slightly, his hand was instantly on it, pressing hard and keeping it down. The stupid whore then had the cheek to make him slow down to exactly thirty. He moved right up to her bumper, arms and scalp tingling angrily. Fucking women drivers. Every second she delayed him made him more annoyed. He stared malevolently at the long curls until a wider section of road opened up ahead then snapped his indicator down to overtake – once he was alongside she'd regret ever scraping through her poxy driving test. He couldn't believe it – she actually accelerated, making him pull in again. Then, to his delight, the lights ahead turned red and he seized his chance. He pulled up behind the car, opened his door and climbed out. His principles prevented him from actually laying a finger on a female. But that didn't mean, in exceptional circumstances, he couldn't rip into them verbally. Right, bitch, he thought, prepare to cry. Then, to his surprise, her door opened too.

The figure climbed quickly out and swept back a mane of blonde hair. Fuck, he hadn't seen a haircut like that on a bloke since Pringle jumpers and sovereign rings. The face was sharp, the nose nothing more than two flattened lumps. He instantly recognised the fighter's ability in the wiry frame, in the way he stepped up, head slightly dipped, ready on the balls of his feet. Dave's step faltered and the man raised his hands and beckoned with his fingers.

'Come on then, you big fuck, try it.'

Cars were pulling up alongside, hemming him in. He stopped and a gust of trepidation caused his anger to collapse like a stack of cards.

'I . . . I thought you were a mate of my wife's. What are you on about?'

'No you didn't, you cunt. You were having a go, so come on.'

'I wasn't – I thought you were someone else,' he insisted with playground obstinacy.

The man's mouth curled in contempt. 'You fucking shitter. Get back to your weights and keep off the fucking road.'

The comment blew a hole clean through him and he turned away, feigning confusion, as the other man started laughing derisively.

By the time he'd fumbled with his seat belt the lights had turned to green and the Micra had disappeared. Shakily, he rolled across the junction and pulled up in the first available side street. The radio blared on.

'The roadworks on the M1 at junction 28 are causing some very long delays, the back of the queue is now somewhere past junction 33. There are severe delays on the M2 north of Belfast as only one lane is open each

way at junction 6 at Antrim. Thanks to Doug and Jimmy who called from Northamptonshire. The southbound A43 is blocked by an accident just outside Towcester. Northbound is open but traffic in the area is severely congested. Thanks for the calls from the M40 heading into London. The police say traffic is crawling from about junction 4. There's no real reason they can see other than the sheer weight of traffic. On the M25 in Essex the roadmenders have hit a snag and only one clockwise lane is open at the moment between junctions 29 and 30, the A127 and the A13 intersections . . .'

Suddenly Dave grabbed the tuning knob on the side of the radio and ripped it clean off. The reception was lost and he began smashing the cylinder into the dial face, splintering the plastic and denting the display.

Chapter 12
The Searcher

He breathed in the books' aroma and ran a hand lovingly over their spines. His fingers lingered at another and he slipped it off the shelf and carefully placed it on the pile in his other arm. That should do, he decided. He looked for an empty table and saw one off to the side by the quietly purring aquarium. It was built into the partition wall that separated the main reading area from the children's section with its bean bags and play mats. He quite liked the particular table he was heading for because it allowed him to gaze through the water at the shimmering shapes of the happy children beyond. Delicately he moved between the tables and chairs, scrupulously avoiding them to maintain the sacred hush.

Once he was sitting down he arranged the various volumes in a protective ring on the table around him. Then he removed his sketch of the orchid-like flower he'd plucked on the central reservation during the night and placed it on the table. He slid *Flora of the British Isles* to the space in front of him and lifted the outer cover, letting it overbalance and catching it before the edge connected with the deeply polished table-top.

But the aquarium caught his eye and he watched the larger fish as they made tiny fluttering adjustments with their fins. Beautifully lit by the lid-mounted tube, one worked its lower jaw up and down and his mind went back to the traffic which had pinned him down a few hours before.

He couldn't tell what caused it, but as soon as the cars started to slow, he'd flattened himself into the long grass and lain perfectly still. Gradually it all stopped moving and he observed the stationary vehicles from a distance of about twelve feet. From the darkness inside one a cigarette periodically glowed; from another the blurred sound of a radio reached his ears. The car nearest to him was an estate, and after a couple of minutes the interior light went on to help the lady in the back locate something on the seat next to her. As she rummaged around, unwittingly on show, oblivious to everything outside the dark glass of the brightly windowed box she was in, her mouth silently moved as she chatted to the pair in front. He wondered what she'd do if he suddenly reared up at the window, hands and face squashed against the glass, lips and tongue sucking at the surface like the underside of a shellfish. But then the light went off and the show ended. Just before the line started moving again the window of the car in front lowered and a hand emptied the contents of an ashtray out on to the tarmac at the edge of the grass. Once the queue had dispersed he wriggled over, stretched out an arm and picked up one of the crushed filters. By his torch he read the word 'Piccadilly'. A new brand that instantly earned a place in his collection.

He shied away from the carefully modulated whisper by his side: 'Sorry to disturb you, sir.' He stared, wide-eyed, at the woman. 'We're conducting a customer survey about the services here at Central Library. I wonder if you could find time to complete some questions.' His eyes turned to the card as she placed it gently on the table at his elbow. 'It will only take a few minutes, and it could help with our council funding for next year.' He turned his head to the form and nodded in hesitant agreement. 'Thank you ever so much,' she said and moved off to another table. Through his alarm he looked at the card and immediately saw the words 'Name' and 'Address'. He knew he would never fill it in: doing so only invited further unwanted contact. Her intrusion had shattered his inner calm, it was against the rules asking questions like that. It went against the very reason he spent so much time here: no one was meant to speak to him in the library.

Chapter 13
The Hunter

'Every job has to have its perks, and this is my favourite. It's like Grandma's fucking Footsteps,' said Walker from the side of his mouth. Their patrol car sat in the middle lane doing precisely 69 m.p.h., traffic backed up behind them. Drivers a few cars away, unable to see what was causing the delay, were pushing dangerously close to the bumpers of the ones in front. One by one vehicles tiptoed past their patrol car, some doing 71 m.p.h., some even 72. 'I love it! They don't dare look at us, even though you can tell they're well pissed off.' Once the cars were about 30 metres in front they would inch their speeds back up. 'They act like they can't see us, like they don't know they just happen to be pipping 70. But I tell you, if I flicked that siren switch every driver for 100 yards ahead would shit himself and hit the brakes.'

Andy managed a weak smile.

'Which reminds me,' said Walker, pulling a pad of speeding tickets from the driver's door and examining the pen marks on the outer cover, 'we need to book a few on our next shift, get our monthly tally back up to a respectable level.' He dropped the pad back into the door. 'It annoys me, you know – some of these businessmen in their Beemers, Mercs and Jags. You collar them for speeding and you know they could pay the fine there and then with the small change in their pockets. Us and our salaries are nothing to them. We're just a trifling inconvenience, and they let you know that's what they're thinking when they look at you. Do you really want to sign up for years of this?'

Andy leaned his head back against the seat. 'It's not all about speeding tickets though, is it? How many stolen cars have you chased over the years?'

'Car chases?' Walker coughed indignantly. 'I could count them on the fingers of one hand.'

Silence filled the car, and hung there until they parked back at base twenty minutes later. They gathered their stuff together and strode across the car park. 'What about this murder enquiry? We're fully involved in it, and you can't say that's boring.'

Walker snorted. 'We've had our look-in on that one. He'll never strike in the same place again. The only thing that case means for us is extra shifts. We'll be sat there in the wee small hours getting piles while he just bides his time.' As they pushed through the canteen doors Walker glanced at his colleague and noticed his deflated expression with satisfaction. 'And when he does get caught,' he carried on, all traces of bitterness removed from his voice for the benefit of those around, 'it won't be because of the likes of us. It'll be video or forensics. Our increased presence is just a PR exercise – isn't that right, Phil?' A man looked up from the table they now stood by. 'All these extra night shifts – we stand more chance of winning the Lottery than catching him.'

'Oooh, yesss,' the man replied with exaggerated gravity. 'He'll have to kill again before we get any closer. Just have to hope he makes a mistake, or runs out of luck.'

Walker took a seat and looked up at Andy who now stood with shoulders sagging. 'You sticking around for a beer?' he asked good-naturedly.

'No, thanks, I'll pass if that's all right. I'm feeling a bit knackered.'

'Righto – see you next shift then,' Walker replied, teasing the sports section out from under the other man's paper. Seeing the conversation was over, Andy set off to the locker room.

'I don't know what's up with him,' said Walker casually, examining the headlines.

The other man replied without looking up, 'What, not taking the pace too well, is he?'

'Mmm, I think he needs a bit more general experience. I don't agree with this skipping all your attachments to do just one.'

The other man raised his head. 'Is that what he's doing?'

'Yeah – didn't you know?' said Walker, knowing he didn't. 'He's got this job on the brain. Doesn't want to know about anything else. It's a bit of a . . . bit of a . . . whatdoyoucallit?'

'Obsession?'

'Yeah, that's it, an obsession.'

He leaned back, satisfied. He'd planted the seed in the canteen itself, the most fertile part of the entire building.

In the locker room Andy hung up his jacket and neon waist jacket on their pegs, rolled up his sleeves and took the pot of gel off the top shelf. Bending towards his mum's old make-up mirror, he tousled his hair from its side parting into something more messy. Then, after wiping his fingers clean with a paper towel, he put his jacket on and headed home. Back at his front door he turned the key quickly in the lock so it made the least amount of noise. Inside the house was quiet. He locked the door, and paused in the hallway with his eyes shut, gauging how tired he felt. Not very. So, instead of climbing the stairs, he stepped lightly into the front room and switched on the light. A note on the table, written in his mother's hand, read, 'Gone to bed. Cold chicken in the fridge. Sleep well. Love, Mum and Derek.' He pulled off his shoes, pushed the door shut and opened the telly guide. Nothing worth watching. He went over to the shelf of video tapes and walked his fingers along the top of the cases, stopping at *Bullitt*.

Every click of the machine seemed extra loud as he loaded up the tape. With one finger ready on the volume control he pressed 'Play' and as soon as the video started turned the sound down so he could just hear it. Collapsed on the sofa, he fast-forwarded to the car chase, letting off the button just at the point where McQueen appeared on the crest of the hill, perfectly framed in the rear-view mirror of the killers' car. Their tyres yelped and the saloon barrelled off to the left in a cloud of smoke. The jazz track cut and for the next ten minutes the only sound was that of the two cars' engines as they revved, roared and raced.

Gunning his squat motor along, McQueen kept in cool pursuit, masterfully carving out wide turns on the broad San Francisco streets. Andy sat transfixed by the scene, left fingers twitching on the cushion beside him with every gear change. Again he noted the appearance once too often of the green Volkswagen Beetle as the two cars slammed their way down the steep-flat-steep streets until they were out of the city and racing along the freeway, recklessly weaving through the oncoming traffic. His fist clenched in satisfaction as McQueen finally rammed the two criminals clean off the road, straight to their agonising death within the flames of the gas station forecourt they ripped into.

He knew Walker was deliberately doing the job down, trying to make it appear mundane, like a waste of time. Walker didn't realise its potential, that was all. He'd grown old and couldn't see all the advantages. But Andy hadn't forgotten real boredom – he was stacking shelves in his local supermarket only five months ago. And if his application to the police force hadn't been accepted, he'd probably still be stacking them now.

Chapter 14
The Killer

The woman gave him a tight-lipped smile and pushed the book back under the Perspex screen. 'OK, Mr Budgen, good luck with your job search and I'll see you again in a fortnight.'

He bowed forward unnecessarily to retrieve his signing-on book and allowed a slightly forlorn note to enter his voice. 'Yeah, thanks.'

With the role of someone wronged over for another two weeks, he got to his feet and turned around. In the queue behind him only the men who looked old enough to retire showed any signs of life. Everyone else waiting their turn in the bare plastic chairs had adopted the same dejected pose. Like people in a doctor's waiting room, none of them kept eye contact for more than a second. Dave picked up his kit bag and walked past the notice boards, half covered with empty promises of interesting work.

Back on the street he straightened up and quickened his pace. Missing his session with Jeff the other day had left tension bunched in his muscles; he was badly in need of a workout. He strode swiftly along, mind on the routine with Jeff that lay ahead, totally unprepared for the bus shelter poster advertising the 'New! Rainbow Whirl Ice Lolly'. The little girl's delighted eyes cut through his thoughts and nearly did the same to his legs. Quickly he angled his head towards the row of shop windows to his right, scanning the products with jaw clenched tight until he was safely round the corner. Every time his eyes locked with the candid stare of some little girl it seemed to burn the image of the eyes he didn't want to see ever again deeper into his mind. And he couldn't bear it.

In the gym he found his training partner waiting for him in the big seat by the TV. As Dave neared the set he could see some dire day-time discussion on the screen. People sat around in a fake-looking lounge/studio setting, earnestly talking. 'For fuck's sake, get this,' his mate said. 'They're giving advice on what to do if you break down now.' He began to mimic the female presenter's soft Irish accent. 'Wait for the rescue vehicle inside your car with the doors locked. I thought you were meant to wait outside your car?' he asked the screen. Dave stood behind, silently watching.

The woman carried on, 'When help arrives, ask to see identification before unlocking your doors . . .'

'What a load of crap!' Jeff interrupted, getting to his feet. They clasped hands. 'How's tricks?' he asked.

'Not bad, mate. I've got some energy to burn off in here, though.'

'OK, let's get on with it. By the way, Gav's probably in later. If we see him I'll mention the all-nighter, if you're still on for it?'

'Too right.'

They entered the main gym area and crossed immediately to the far corner. Squatting there was the biggest machine in the room. Its angular metal frame was bent back on itself so it seemed that, at any moment, it was about to spring straight and send the 20kg discs piled on its stubby arms spinning across the room. Without waiting to be asked Dave folded himself into the horizontal seat and raised the soles of his feet up to the metal plates.

'Bit eager today, mate,' said Jeff.

'Like I said – got energy to burn.'

Pushing against the foot-plates, he raised the load clear of the supporting hooks and turned them out of the way by adjusting two handles at his hips. He then allowed the foot-plates to slide slowly down the two oily poles. Once his knees were pressed up against his chest he reversed the descent, pushing his legs straight. The plates slid slowly back up. Jeff stood to the side doing some light stretches, waiting his turn. Some fifty minutes and two other leg exercises later, their routine was over. Both men were flushed and shiny.

'Fuck, you were hammering it today,' said Jeff, rubbing his burning thighs with thick fingers.

'And I'm not finished yet. Fancy a session on the punch bag?' Dave asked, massaging the sides of his aching jaw with one hand.

Jeff raised his eyebrows at this break in routine. 'No, you're all right. I want to be able to get out of bed tomorrow.'

Dave let out a short laugh. 'All right, I'm going to do a few minutes, I'll see you in the lounge.' He walked over to the mirrored side room where the punch bag hung on a hook like a huge slab of red meat. He shut the door behind him. Stepping up to it, he took a quick breath and then launched at it with both fists. The chain danced and jumped as, with feet rooted to the spot and all rhythm and aim lost, he lashed at it in a frenzy. Sharp nasal bursts accompanied each blow; snot flew from his face. Every so often he would pause just long enough to gulp in breath and then the onslaught would begin again. Within a few minutes his shoulders and upper arms felt red hot. Gravity increased so that it became harder and harder to land punches at head height. Soon he was leaning forward, forehead against the bag, pummelling weaker and weaker blows at a stomach-high spot. And then he gave up, both arms hugging the bag as he gasped and sobbed into the thick red plastic.

When he walked unsteadily back into the lounge area, Jeff was at a table chatting with a man wearing a baggy white tracksuit and a crimson bandanna around his bald head. An untouched glass of milkshake stood on the table.

'Dave, this is Gav. Runs the security at the Shebeen and a few other places round town,' said Jeff. Dave had frequently seen the man in the gym, but they'd never spoken until now.

Gav hardly raised his head, just looked up at Dave from under a heavy-boned brow. When he spoke his voice was surprisingly high. 'Jeff's mentioned it, yeah? I could do with some extra hands for this all-nighter coming up.'

Dave sat down. 'Yeah, he did. I'm up for it, no problem. Just give us the details.'

'Right, we've just got to fill in this form. All the clubs have to use doormen who are part of a registered agency. Some bollocks council ruling.' He pulled a plastic folder from his training bag and took a sheet of paper from it. 'This is my agency – Peacemakers. Like it?' Dave looked at the top of the form with its smoking gun logo and smiled. Gav popped a ball-point pen open.

'Surname?'

'My real one?'

'Fuck that, just make one up.'

'I don't know. Who are you?' he asked, looking at Jeff for help.

'Fucked if I remember. Johnson, was it?'

'OK. I'll be Jones.'

'Don't, for fuck's sake,' said Gav, 'give me a Christian name of Jack. You'll sound like a cockney twat.'

They all laughed. 'No,' Dave said. 'Make it Arnie – he kicks arse, right, Jeff?'

'Too right.'

'OK,' said Gav, 'Arnie Jones. Address?'

'Erm – I don't know. 90b Ginsley Terrace.'

'Date of birth?'

'Seventh of the fourth, sixty-six.' It was beginning to feel like an appointment at the dole office. 'This is all cash in hand, yeah?'

Gav looked up. 'Sure. The only people who'll see this is us three and the club owner. Any convictions?'

'Just robbing a few cars years ago.'

'I'm not really asking, mate. Just say none.'

Dave was getting confused. 'None.'

'Thought so,' said Gav, crossing the relevant box. 'Nice one – just sign Arnie Jones there and I'll fill in the other bits.'

Dave scrawled a signature at the bottom and Gav put the paper back in the folder. 'OK, it's Saturday after next. Eleven o'clock start, so be there for 10.30. Eight pounds an hour and we kick 'em out at 7 a.m.' As he told Dave the details he wrote them down on a business card. 'There you go, it's all here.'

'Cheers,' Dave said, putting the card in his kit bag. 'This mine?' he asked, picking up the drink. Jeff nodded. As he knocked it back the other two began talking about the coming weekend's football. Once his glass was empty he put it back on the table and looked at Jeff. 'I've got to get off, see you Monday?'

'No problem.'

'OK. Cheers for the job, Gav – I'll see you around.'

As he stood, Gav did too and they clasped hands. 'Safe,' said Gav, winking as he sat back down. Once Dave was gone he turned to Jeff. 'What's he like – can he handle himself?'

'To be honest, I'm not sure, mate,' Jeff replied. 'I've done a few pub nights with him, but nothing's ever happened. There's something about him, though. Something . . .' He struggled to put a finger on what he was trying to say. 'Give him a flying jacket and a head mike and he looks the part, though. Have him on the front doing searches with me if you're not one hundred per cent sure.'

Dave pushed open his front door and listened. No sounds of kids' TV, just a rustling of plastic bags.

'Is that you, Dave? I'm in here!' called his wife from the kitchen.

He looked in at Sally putting shopping into the fridge. 'Where's Jasmine?' he asked.

'At her grandma's – like she is most Wednesday afternoons.'

'God, of course. I always forget,' he replied, dropping his kit bag down in front of the washing machine. 'Can you give that lot a spin? It's humming.'

She sighed. 'Yes – once I put the shopping away. Have you got any jobs on this afternoon?'

'Nope,' relied Dave with some relief – his arms were still quivering from his work-out. 'We can watch a film on satellite if you want.'

'Good idea – that new Hugh Grant one is showing every half an hour. Let's do that. You, me and a nice cuddle on the sofa.'

'Sounds good, I'll grab a quick shower.'

She screwed up the last of the bags and pressed them into a drawer already full from previous shopping trips. Then she turned her attention to his kit bag, sliding the zip open and lifting the damp vest out. She pressed it to her face and shut her eyes, breathing in the sharp smell of sweat. Flicking open the washing machine, she began throwing the various items of kit inside, stopping when a business card fell out on to the floor.

She looked at the simple image of the Western-style gun for a moment. 'Peacemakers,' she mouthed, turning it over and reading the date and times written on the back. Her eyes paused at the pound sign. 'Eight pounds an hour,' she whispered out loud with a smile, before slipping the card back into the bag.

Chapter 15
The Searcher

The recent sunny weather had made the air in his house grow dry and stale. He never opened the windows in any of his rooms because to do so meant parting the thick muslin sheets hanging across them; and doing that would give someone on the street, or in the houses opposite, a glance at his collection. The most he would ever move the sheeting was approximately five centimetres apart, and this was solely for the purpose of allowing a shaft of sunlight through in order to study certain finds. He sat on a chair in the middle of the room reserved for 'items of a biodegradable nature not thrown from vehicles'. Miniature towers of Perspex and glass jars loomed in the half-light all around him. They were piled on his shelves, filled all his drawers and spilled out towards the centre of the room.

The slant of white light shining in through the slit crossed his lap. Balanced there was a container. Held before his face and bisecting the beam was another, containing his specimen of *Ortherum cancellatum*. Despite the airtight lid, decomposition had set in. The compound eyes, now dull and lifeless, had partially collapsed, the legs had curled under the abdomen and the brittle wings had splintered and cracked. A long, sad sigh escaped him. Placing it carefully on the floorboards at his side, he picked up the next container with more care. This one was full of liquid, cider vinegar to be precise. Hanging in the faintly yellow fluid was the burst remains of *Natrix natrix*, recovered from his last forage. He had kept it because the head was intact, milky reptilian eyes open. Innards drifted downwards like bunches of bleached rubber bands. He observed its precise camouflage, noting how the row of markings running down the snake's side spread across individual scales so that some were a two-tone black and green. Like the dragonfly, the creature also was bound by cycles, shedding its skin and hibernating at regular intervals over its twenty-year or so life-span. He wondered what sort of instinct decided that those exact scales developed both colours so that its overall pattern remained so regular.

Into the hush of the room crept faint voices – excited and high. They were outside on the street and getting nearer. He lowered the jar and tilted his head fractionally to one side. The light scrape of trainers below let him know they were now on his front path. Whispers and suppressed giggles completely betrayed their attempts at stealth. He sat motionless, listening.

The flap of the letterbox slowly creaked open and something bounced on to the hallway floor. Giggles erupted into breathless laughter and quick footsteps carried the sounds away. The low summery sounds of birds singing and music faintly playing slowly reasserted themselves. He watched the dust motes swarming in the beam before his face. Tiny fragments of fibre and dots of nothing that tumbled slowly or slid sideways in the still air, their movements controlled by forces too slight for him to sense. Maybe affected by heat from his own body. Delicately he parted his lips and blew out a thin stream of air. The dust caught in the immediate blast vanished instantly into the darkness beyond the light's sharp edge. Surrounding specks surged at the moving air, like ants attacking a threat to the nest. They vanished too, as did their neighbours, in an unending convergence that only finished when he ran out of breath. He sucked in air, picturing all the particles now being drawn into his lungs, and stood.

The grass snake went back into the section dedicated to *Reptilia*, the dragonfly to a larger section reserved for insects. The box slid in amongst the stacks of beetles, bees and butterflies. He stepped lightly down the stairs and, as the doormat came into view, saw the half-full bottle lying on its side. The rest of its contents lay in a mostly absorbed puddle across his carpet. Picking it up, he sniffed the moist neck and his nostrils filled with the tang of urine. Why was the tool of torment so often urine? he wondered. It was the same at the care home. The first time it had happened he'd been in the reading room. He spent most evenings browsing through the sad collection of books that lined the shelves. Rejects and unwanteds from charity shops or church jumble sales with the pencilled price still visible on the inside front cover. Often next to older inscriptions featuring unusual or extinct names. 'Property of Herbert Lyle, Form 3.' 'To Eunice, Happy Christmas from Aunty Hermione.' Sometimes he found these handwritten addendums more thought-provoking than the stories, trying to picture the previous owners and what sort of lives other people led.

They'd come bustling through the swing doors, filling the empty room with furtive whispers, and he'd watched from the corner of his eye as they positioned themselves at the other end of the table. The same suppressed giggles. One by one they took swigs from their cans with overdone stealth, waiting for him to react, to ask what they were doing. He kept his eyes moving back and forth across the page before him, watching them all the while. Eventually they were forced to attract his attention with a 'Pssssst'. He looked up. The can was being held out to him, below the level of the table top. The invitation to try some. Despite his learned wariness a part of him still hoped the offer was the start of acceptance, even friendship. He would have gladly drunk or sniffed anything for that. He closed the book and moved down the table, taking a seat and the passed can. They watched with delight as he sipped the sweet, warm liquid. Then with disbelieving glee as he took another, more confident gulp. Two of them burst into triumphant roars while the third gasped, 'It's piss! It's piss!'

They'd jumped up, clutching their cans, and staggered laughing from the room, all friends together. But he didn't know what beer tasted like. Didn't know, until then, what piss tasted like either.

He walked into the kitchen, emptied the remains down the sink and placed the empty bottle on the window sill along with all the others.

Chapter 16
The Hunter

'Wakey wakey, pal!' Andy's eyes opened with a start. Walker's fat gut filled most of his vision. As he blinked he could see various other officers dotted around the canteen grinning and shaking their heads. The newspaper was hanging off the edge of the table, the middle pages had slid on to his lap. 'Time to go out and catch some bad guys,' Walker added, a smile tipping the corners of his mouth upwards.

Clumsily, Andy refolded the paper. 'Shit, I can't believe I fell asleep. How long was I sat like that for?' he asked, following Walker between the tables.

'Oh, not too long,' replied Walker over his shoulder. The casual way he said it made Andy feel uneasy.

The central locking on their patrol car for the night clicked and they climbed in, the seats feeling cold through their uniform. 'Did any senior officers see me?' asked Andy.

'No – I'd have woken you if anyone important had come in,' Walker lied. 'But you looked so comfy sat there. Snoring.'

'I wasn't, was I? You're kidding me?'

Walker just cackled as he started the engine. 'Right, we're covering Bravo stretch on the M40 tonight. East or west end? West is best, I reckon.'

The car purred along, the light inside it continually building up and dying away as they sped beneath the motorway lamps away from the city. Once they got to the signs for the services they'd shared a coffee at several weeks before, Walker turned off, swung the patrol car round the roundabout and then rejoined the motorway going in the opposite direction. After a few miles they passed the pile of flowers marking the spot where the girl had disappeared. A couple of minutes further on he slowed up and pulled on to the hard shoulder. He manoeuvred the vehicle up the concealed ramp and turned the engine and lights off. Clicking sounds filled the car as the engine slowly cooled.

'Ten to bastard six. God, I hate night shifts,' sighed Walker heavily.

Andy leaned back in the seat, digging his nails into its leather-effect edging. 'Well, we could always play I Spy.'

Rather than smile, Walker sagged further down into his seat. Their customary silence draped itself impenetrably around them once again. Every so often the radio would crackle a message out to colleagues on the night shift. After a while Walker's slow breathing attracted Andy's attention and he turned his head to look at him. In the privacy of their patrol car it was the older man's turn to sleep.

Chapter 17
The Killer

Apparently Leeds was getting to be quite a nice place, not that he could tell. One industrial park was much like another, and all were located in that characterless belt of land that rings every town or city.

As he dropped down from the motorway flyover he could see into a breaker's yard below him. Chained shut for the night, the premises lay quiet, free from any activity. Stacked on top of each other in precarious-looking piles were masses of cars. The ring of floodlights glaring down on the grim arena clearly illuminated the uppermost vehicles. Many looked pretty much undamaged; their only visible fault seemed to be their boxy lines and outdated styling. Condemned for looking wrong. Next to these piles were the concentrated remains of countless others, their bodies reduced and compacted into cubes of sheet metal. Watching over them were several monstrous vehicles, long necks outstretched, open jaws poised above the motionless remains. As if waiting for movement before striking cruelly down.

In the middle of the yard, surrounded by fragments of metal and shreds of tyres, sat a crusher. The floodlights lit up its battered and scratched sides, leaving the square pit in the middle cast in dark shadow. The crude processing site, with its razor-wire outer fencing, brought another faint image to Dave's mind. A similar fortress, only with a railway leading through its outer gates to squat chimneyed buildings in its centre.

He descended the ramp and looked beyond the carnage of the yard to the next floodlit premises. This expanse was much larger, filled with row upon row of pristine cars. Parked in scrupulously ordered blocks of colour, the vehicles awaited shipment to a network of garages. And from there they would enter the road system for a brief time before finishing up at the place he'd just passed. The chequered ranks sat patiently around a flat-roofed, prefabricated block: the factory he was aiming for.

He'd dropped the parts off no problem, parking round the back of the monstrous warehouse and carrying them into the loading area himself. The evening supervisor had signed for them and, amongst the exhaust fumes of reversing lorries, invited Dave into the building for a meal in the staff canteen. He'd turned it down and, instead, climbed back into his van and opened up his road atlas of Great Britain. As he studied the network of roads he rubbed the sides of his jaw with one hand – the ache seemed to be taking root, penetrating deep into the hinge itself.

He decided to head east, up the M62, then skirt round on a southerly arc and see what he could find. Automatically, he reached for the button of the radio before remembering he'd ripped off the tuning knob, jamming the reception on a load of static. Instead he slotted his one and only tape – All Time Eighties Classics – into the machine, turned up the volume and set off. It wasn't long before he passed a sign telling him that the approaching services were the last for 38 miles. Perfect. He pulled in to make the necessary changes.

A few minutes later he was passing over the brow of a hill, hunting kit ready on the seat beside him. The motorway stretched off down into the valley below, all six lanes lit up by lamp after lamp after endless lamp. It curled away like a snake, dozens of parallel lights accentuating every kink in the road. The curves reminded him of the trail a sparkler leaves when waved against the night sky. Headlamps of approaching cars created a halo effect on his windscreen, each minute imperfection on its surface twinkling at him as the light passed by. Narrowing his eyes to look at the actual scratches, the motorway lights behind lost their focus, becoming swollen and blurred. Cat's eyes bloated to treble their normal size. He raced onwards, barely able to see which lane he was in, passing headlights shining like distant, hazy beacons in the kaleidoscope of shifting light.

The motorway lights ran out and his way was now lit only by rows of glinting cat's eyes. By shortening his focus still further, perspective was completely lost and everything merged into a glowing lava flow. And then from this shimmering scene the insistent wink of hazard lights broke through.

He blinked once, and as his eyelids peeled back his gaze was once again hard and sharp. No cars behind. Down came the window and on went the siren light. Signalling left, he crossed the markings on to the hard shoulder and pulled up behind the car. He sought the shape of a skull behind the bulky headrests. There was no one in the vehicle. He was just wondering if the person might be stretched out on the back seat asleep when a ring rapped sharply on the passenger window. Startled, he jerked his head round. A woman. Smiling and making winding movements with her hand. A woman. He leaned across and wound down the window.

'Hi, there.' American accent. 'Thank God you're here, my flight leaves in under an hour.'

A woman. This was not what he was looking for. He grabbed the clipboard and pretended to check her registration against the order form for the parts he'd delivered earlier. 'I'm sorry, love, I've got the wrong car. I've been called out for a red Peugeot, but not with your number plate. Mine must be just further round the corner.'

'Oh, Jesus.' She glanced back up the deserted motorway lanes, looking for another vehicle. 'They said half an hour and it's been more than that already.'

He had to get moving. 'Don't worry – it's a quiet night, they'll be here soon.' He pulled off, leaving the solitary figure on the road behind him.

Chapter 18
The Searcher

He dropped his hand and the pages of the calendar flopped back against the kitchen wall. He thought so: it was exactly a month since he'd had to call off his forage because of all the emergency sirens stopping just further down the motorway. He felt pleased at how his mind had worked in a perfect cycle; just like the dragonfly's and grass snake's. It wasn't a conscious decision to return on the night of the full moon but, since his body clock had dictated it, he would. Removing some shopping bags from the kitchen drawer, he set off to retrace his steps to the exact spot he'd parked at before.

In less than forty minutes his light-brown Datsun Stanza stopped on the track. In the darkness he put on his fatigues and went about applying the grass snake's pattern to his face and hands. Next he completed a mental check of all his pockets, locked his car and climbed the fence into the dark field beyond. Immediately his foot sank into a soft wide lump. By looking slightly off to the side, his eyes were able to make out a black shape surrounding his foot. He reached down; a cowpat, cold like blancmange.

He carried on, stepping carefully through the grass, hands held slightly outwards. Somewhere near, a screech owl sounded its regretful cry. Midway across, his hand brushed against a wire fence that hadn't been there before. He listened a few moments for the tick of electricity. Hearing none he squatted down and squeezed through the parallel wires. Just as he was nearing the other side of the field a low breath shuddered out of the night before him. A burst of adrenaline jolted his veins and he had to fight the urge to turn and flee. Straining his eyes ahead he was just able to make out the bulky shapes of some dozing cows. They lay on their sides, legs folded beneath them, chewing the cud and unaware of his presence. He knew that, although harmless, they were prone to crowding round people with a dumb curiosity. So, taking advantage of a break in the traffic, he quickly slipped under the lowest bar of the fence and began crawling sideways down the embankment, looking back to check they hadn't risen to gather behind him.

Andy was intently watching the sporadic bursts of passing cars when the shadowy figure emerged from under the bottom of the fence up on his left. His eyes opened wide. The figure began crawling sideways down the slope, looking back at the fence the whole time. Keeping absolutely still, Andy curled his fingers round the flashlight in the door's compartment and whispered, 'Ray! Ray!' The man didn't stir. 'Ray!' he desperately hissed, glancing at the oblivious mound beside him. 'For fuck's sake.' He reached across to the steering column, switched the headlights on and snapped his door open, simultaneously shouting, 'Oi!' The figure was caught facing the full beam. Andy could see the whites of his eyes against the thick camouflage cream plastering his face. As he leapt from the car Walker was just starting to splutter in confusion.

The white light was suddenly all around him, harsh and unforgiving. For a split second he was totally bewildered, blinking stupidly at the glare. But then the human shout. He was off, scrambling up the slope. The headlamps had burned their imprint on his retinas and all he could see was mushrooming explosions of yellow and red. He ran full into the fence and tumbled over the top. Getting immediately to his feet he glanced to his left, and through the swirling colours saw the light of a torch bobbing quickly towards him. He sprinted into the blackness ahead. With each sightless step he tried to let just the toes of his foot make contact

88

with the lumpy turf, knowing that if he twisted an ankle now he would surely be caught. And then from nowhere an unseen hand stopped him dead in his tracks and flung him full on to his back. Next thing, he was lying stretched out in the thick grass, staring at the night sky. Sounds – human and animal – came from over by the fence and a narrow light-beam swept the air above him.

'What the hell is going on?'

'Fucking animals, get out of the fucking way!'

'What are you doing?'

The beam swung back above him and then carried on.

'He was fucking here, I tell you!'

By slowly inching his chin up, he tilted his head backwards and looked behind him. The silhouettes of two figures were visible, one holding a torch. The cows had struggled to their feet and ambled over to the pair, forming a barrier between him and the probing beam.

'What are you on about?'

'This . . . this man. He came out from under the fence. Full fucking combat gear. Cam-cream all over his face. He was heading for the hard shoulder. Seriously, Ray – I'm not bullshitting you!'

'Where'd he go then?'

'I don't fucking know! I was only thirty metres behind the bastard. These bloody things!' A palm slapped on solid flesh and a cow snorted. 'He just vanished. I don't understand it.'

The mass of cows had now completely blocked his view of the fence.

'Well, let's get back to the car.'

'Shit!'

The voices grew fainter. He wriggled through 180 degrees and moved hesitantly forward. When the thin strand pressed into the top of his head, he pushed it up and crawled through the gap in the taut wire fence. A little further on he stood and jogged carefully to the other side of the field. Abandoning his routine, he reversed back up the track and then drove away from the motorway, out into the empty countryside beyond.

*

The twat hadn't even wound down the frigging window. Just sat on the back seat and pointed Dave towards the left-hand front tyre. Then he'd gone back to speaking into his poxy tape recorder, briefcase open on his lap.

Dave returned to his van wondering what to do. He didn't even have a spare tyre – not for a fucking Jag anyway. And he had no idea when the guy had called for a rescue vehicle. Jesus, this was going wrong. Badly wrong. He got out his jack and tyre irons. As he went back to the car the man tapped on the window.

'Don't worry about me. I'll keep absolutely still.'

Dave nodded obediently, totally unused to having lost control of the situation. He placed the jack under the car, fitted the rod of metal into its side and pumped it until the tyre lifted just clear of the tarmac.

Working quickly, he unwound the nuts and lifted the tyre off. Time ticked by and an idea finally came. He walked slowly round the car, kicking all the other tyres.

They sat staring out of the windscreen.

'We've got to radio for back-up – he can't have got far. It must have been him.'

'Whoa there, cowboy!' said Walker. His condescending tone immediately annoyed Andy. 'Think. If we call in now claiming you've just spotted the Motorway Murderer, we'll have Scotland Yard and every other policeman for God knows how far descending on this place. They'll probably close the motorway – just in time for the morning rush to London. This is a very big call. Are you absolutely sure you saw something?'

Andy lost it. 'Fuck you, Ray – you were fucking asleep, that's why you didn't see anything!'

Now they faced each other.

'Listen very carefully, Seer. I. Was. Not. Asleep. If you blurt out to anyone that I was, I'll make sure your career in the police force is finished before it's even begun. Do you understand?'

Andy stared at him. 'Listen, I'm not trying to drop you in the shit. For God's sake – this is far more important than any snoozing on the job. I saw some freak in army overalls, cam-ed up, creeping down on to the hard shoulder less than three miles away from where he last struck.'

Walker was shitting himself. If this kid went back to the station and started blabbing about spotting the Motorway Murderer – and how his senior colleague had tried to hush it up because he was asleep – he stood to lose everything: including his pension. He saw thirty years of inconsequential service fizzling out in shame and failure. Leaving the station for the last time to a few awkward hand-shakes from those who weren't too embarrassed to acknowledge him. He couldn't let it happen.

Keeping his voice slow and measured, he said, 'Andy, I think you're tired, I think you're stressed and I think you're having problems coping with the job. I seriously advise you to hold back on this, think it over tonight and we'll talk again in the morning. You can have my home number. You will make a good traffic policeman, OK? I don't want you to screw up your chances.'

'So you're not going to radio in?' Andy pressed, desperation making him whine.

'Absolutely not. Let's just get some coffee for now, all right?' said Walker, starting the car, sensing the upper hand.

He knocked politely on the window. The man glanced at him and Dave saw he hadn't stopped the tape recorder. He put on an atrocious Scottish accent. 'Sir, ken ah ask ye when yer tyres were last checked?'

'What?' mouthed the man through the glass, impatiently.

Keeping his voice at speaking level, Dave asked the question again. The man clicked off the tape recorder and wound down the window a fraction. 'What did you say?'

He repeated the question once more.

'I don't know – not that long ago. The company takes care of it.'

'Well, ah'm afraid, sir, yeh've gut a gud case fae suing your employer. All four tyres are completely shut through. Thair've really put yer life at risk letting ye drive this vehicle.'

'You're bloody joking!' the man said, slamming the tape recorder into the briefcase and shoving it on to the seat beside him. 'I knew this bloody company was a bad bet,' he cursed to himself, unlocking the door and getting out, tie flapping in the breeze. 'This tyre's completely bald? Show me,' he demanded, bending forward to peer at the prone tyre. Dave raised the tyre iron high and swung it on a long arc down on to the man's skull.

His legs buckled and he pitched head first into the side of the car before folding on to the ground. Dave looked down at the man, lying on his back before him, and grinned. The force of the blow had knocked one of his eyes out of its socket. Held by the optic nerve, it dangled against his temple, looking towards the ground. The other eye was blinking stupidly up at the night sky and Dave wondered what he could actually see. Half heaven and half hell? Probably nothing.

Carefully he placed the tapered end of the tyre iron into the red pulp of the exposed socket and leaned on it with all his weight. It sank into the man's head and his back arched as if an electrical current were passing through it. As his limbs started thrashing wildly Dave began twisting the rod from side to side and banging on the top of it with the heel of his hand. Eventually he heard the metal tip grinding against the asphalt below.

'Hoos the fat fuckin' cat noo?' He smiled at the slack face. He placed a foot on the man's forehead, pulled the iron out, adjusted his grip, and like a man breaking through ice smashed the end of the tool again and again into the man's upturned face. 'Hoo's the fat fuckin' cat noo!' he shrieked at the corpse.

Walker felt good. He'd coaxed, cajoled and comforted Andy for two hours, working him like a suspect until his beliefs had started to waver. He was pretty certain the lad would keep his mouth shut. He just had to get him off home; they weren't on shift again for another day and a half, and every hour that passed increased his own chances of survival. With slow and deliberate steps he led Andy from the grey pre-dawn of the car park into the sharp lighting of the police station corridor: straight into their senior officer. They stood in a perfect triangle looking at each other, eyebrows raised, waiting for each other to speak.

The tube light above them quietly buzzed as they all started at once.

'Walker . . . Seer, of course, you haven't . . .'

'I've seen him.'

'What's on the menu tonight . . .' Walker's voice trailed away.

'I beg your pardon?' said the Inspector, frowning.

'I saw him tonight at about 2.40 a.m. on the hard shoulder. Bravo stretch, by where the little girl went . . .'

'Andy,' Walker tried to butt in, 'I think we should discuss this in private . . .'

'He was wearing army fatigues, camouflage cream, the lot. He was there, waiting.'

'Andy,' Walker implored.

Andy rounded on him. 'Just shut up, will you? I'm not keeping quiet on this one.' He turned to his Inspector. 'Ray was asleep – he missed everything. But I saw him, I got a good look. Enough for an e-fit.'

Both men looked at Walker. He dropped his eyes to the floor in defeat.

'I think we'd better talk in my office,' said the Inspector abruptly. They followed him in silence, Walker between the other two men like someone being led to his execution.

As soon as the door shut the Inspector began. 'Sit down, both of you. First thing, he's killed again. A74, north of Carlisle. The report came in around an hour ago. We didn't radio cars out on patrol because we didn't want any hackers tipping off the press any sooner than they'll find out anyway.' Walker and Seer looked at him in astonishment. 'Now what the hell were you gibbering about in the corridor?'

Seer had turned to stone. Walker lifted himself in his seat. 'Sir, I didn't think there was any need to report it. We were parked up on a concealed ramp, Andy had nodded off. Next thing he's jumping out of the car, screaming that he'd seen something in the dark. I was trying to get him to go home, sleep on it and maybe see a stress counsellor – he was getting hysterical.'

The older men regarded each other steadily.

'You bastard,' Andy whispered. 'He was asleep, not me. This is impossible – I saw him.'

The Inspector went over to a wall map of Great Britain. Red pins marked the sites of all the killings so far – including the latest one. He measured the distance between where the last two murders had occurred. 'Unless your man ran to his car and averaged 140 m.p.h. up the M40, M42, M6 and A74, I can't see how he managed it.'

'It's true – I swear. Walker's been lying all along,' Andy said, his voice getting louder. 'I saw the broken-down car on the M40 as well, but he made me keep quiet about that too . . .'

'Enough!' the Inspector barked.

Walker's breath seeped out and relief flooded through to his very fingertips. He was off the gallows and it was Andy who now stood on the trap door, rope about his neck.

'Jeremy,' Walker interrupted, 'we've all been under a heck of a lot of stress. It's nothing a bit of rest for the lad won't see right.' Ever the professional he switched topics to the case itself, at the same time demonstrating a generous willingness to forget his partner's accusations. 'Were there any witnesses to this latest one?'

'No – but I'll brief you personally in due course. I don't think we need you any more, Ray, you get off home.'

Walker nodded and got to his feet. As he turned, he placed a sympathetic hand on Andy's shoulder. It was instantly shrugged off.

Once they were alone the Inspector began to speak. 'OK, Constable Seer. What you came out with just now was a statement serious enough to have a man suspended, probably sacked. Obstructing a murder investigation. Impeding a witness. I want you to know that Sergeant Walker is just two months short of thirty years' service. Every bit of it exemplary. You, on the other hand, have none. Now putting aside the fact that, as far as I know, killers haven't yet developed the power of flight, it hasn't escaped my notice that you were asleep in the canteen at the start of your shift tonight.'

Andy felt sick. The sound of the other man's voice began to slur in his head. The Inspector walked back to his desk and picked up a thin folder.

'As a matter of fact,' he went on, his voice now softer, 'I was just looking at your file. I notice under your medical notes that you've already seen your family GP about an inability to sleep when you were under stress.'

Andy looked at him without comment.

'Ray is right – we're all under a lot of pressure. And you, perhaps, have had too much thrust upon you, too soon. You've been doing plenty of extra shifts for a start, haven't you?'

Andy nodded.

'You know, it's a funny thing, shift work. It messes with your body clock. Takes a lot of getting used to. Did you know we police officers tend to die younger than the population as a whole? They think it's due to years of shift work. Now I can't have officers out on patrol suffering from exhaustion or stress, so I'm going to sign you off for a few weeks' sick leave. I want you to go home and take it easy, and when you come back I want you to see a police counsellor about your sleep problems. I assume you're still experiencing them?'

Andy nodded.

'OK. I see little point in taking this further, and you can count yourself lucky that Ray is kind enough to think the same. I'll contact you soon about when you can return to duty. Until then, stay at home and try to rest.'

Like a zombie, Andy lifted himself out of his seat and shuffled from the room.

Chapter 19
The Searcher

He couldn't work out where they were coming from, the dozens of bristly bluebottles that buzzed thickly around his house. For the first day after the chase he'd been too unsettled, too scared, to do anything but lie in his bed. Every time a car door slammed or he heard loud, official-sounding voices on the street below, he cowered there, waiting for the inevitable bang on his door. What did they mean when they said 'He was here.' How did they know? Had they been watching him, spying from their hiding places on the edge of his foraging grounds? Why couldn't people just leave him alone?

At first he'd just watched the flies as they entered his bedroom, freshly hatched and full of life. They would search the room with jagged changes of direction, occasionally settling on his sheets to rub their spidery forelegs against each other and preen their little wings. Then they'd take off again until, by chance, their flight path would carry them back out of the open door. By the next day the inside of the house had lost its appeal and they began to yearn for the dim light at the sheeted windows. They crawled behind the material and bounced their hard bodies repeatedly against the unyielding surface.

Eventually hunger forced him from his bed. He climbed out, put his shoes back on and walked carefully down the stairs. A few tins in the kitchen, more flies swarming at the window. Working the tin opener was almost impossible – when he'd been thrown on to his back by the fence he must have jarred his wrist. Now it would hardly bend at all. He ate food cold from the can and when he swung the lid of the bin open more flies rose up from inside. He emptied the contents on to the kitchen floor. Wrappers and containers, but no maggots. The flies' droning, uninvited presence started to aggravate him.

He'd begun searching his trophy rooms, first checking 'items of a biodegradable nature thrown from vehicles'. Holding up the containers in the shaft of light he'd studied the remains for signs of life. Fossilised burgers, withered banana skins, shrunken apple cores, entire tins of sweets, furred remains of sausage rolls. The lids were all on tight, seals unbroken. Back upstairs he searched 'items of a biodegradable nature not thrown from vehicles'. He pulled stacks of Perspex containers into the centre of the room and peered inside. Broken and wasted animal remains lay behind the clear plastic – the only maggots were long dead, dry like grains of rice.

The pain in his wrist throbbed at a constant level, worsening when he had to use his hand for even the smallest task. The skin was swollen and becoming discoloured by the beginnings of an ugly bruise. Another day passed and he knew there was only one thing to do; the leaflet in the library had informed him long ago that the Albert Hospital 'boasts the latest in medical equipment and an efficient service delivered by our friendly team of medical professionals'.

He walked nervously through the sliding doors and looked around the reception area. It was arranged in a series of horseshoe shapes facing each other. He searched for any chairs off to the sides, away from other people. There were none. Reluctantly he walked over to the least full section, sat down and began to examine the pattern on the floor at his feet. Every so often a name would be called out. After a while he risked a quick glance up and saw the voice was coming from a desk, one side marked 'Appointments', the other 'Injuries less than three days old'. A woman in a white dress would return every so often, look at the computer screen and call out a name. The person would go over and the woman would write their name in one of two books and then usher them through into a curtained-off area. He would have to get his name in one of the books. He waited until no one else was at the desk and then walked hesitantly over. The nurse returned.

Briskly she asked, 'Can I help you?' Her voice echoed in the cavernous hall.

'A more-than-three-days-old injury. Please,' he whispered.

'Sorry – you have an injury that you sustained more than three days ago?' she asked, trying to make eye contact. He kept his gaze directed at the counter top and nodded.

'What's the name of the doctor who referred you?' she said, forefinger poised over the keyboard. The question confused him. He'd only had a doctor when he was much younger, and couldn't remember his name. The silence behind him grew louder. He shrugged his shoulders.

'You don't remember the name of the doctor who's referred you? Did he give you any sort of a referral note?'

He shook his head, wrist throbbing at his side.

'Are you registered with a doctor in the city?' Her voice was getting louder. Always questions. Always wanting to know things. The blood burned in his ears and he knew everyone behind was staring at his back. 'To receive treatment for an injury over three days old,' she went mercilessly on, 'we must have a referral from your doctor. The Park Clinic is very close. If you need to register with one I suggest you go there.'

Forms. More questions. Letters landing on his doormat asking him things. Miserably he stood there, unsure of what to say next. 'Excuse me, I have to attend . . .' She walked stiffly away, the sentence trailing off to nothing. He was left stranded, his back riddled by sight lines from everyone behind him. His fingertips fell from the edge of the counter and he started quickly for the sliding doors. As the smoked glass moved apart he darted for the gap – almost straight into the massive figure on the other side.

Chapter 20
The Killer

The smelly little prick somehow managed to twist round him, then was gone. He stepped into the entrance hall, saw the desks and strode over. A nurse emerged from behind a screened-off area. 'Can I help you?' she asked.

'Yeah – please. I've got an 11.30 booking with the physio. Mr Budgen,' he said, holding out his appointment card.

'OK, sir, you've actually come into Casualty. If you head for the corridor on my left, just follow the wall signs for Physiotherapy. It's about two minutes down there.'

Feeling slightly sheepish, he thanked her and set off down the corridor. The marble-effect floor was spotless; trolleys with the ill and injured rolled silently over it, pushed by cotton-suited orderlies. He passed youngsters on crutches and pensioners in wheelchairs, and their injuries sent a writhing sensation up his spine. After a while he got to some double doors marked 'Physiotherapy'.

Pushing through, he entered a small waiting room. More old people sat dotted around, most in pairs. A woman smiled at him from a hatch in the wall. He handed his appointment card over and took a seat while the couples around him talked quietly to each other. He looked with distaste at the pile of dog-eared magazines on the table next to him and pushed the top ones back with the tip of one finger, not wanting actually to pick up a magazine for women. After a few minutes a door opened at the other end of the room and a voice called out, 'Mr Budgen?'

He quickly stood up. The girl was holding the door open for him. She seemed too young to understand medicine. He walked across and she showed him into a curtained-off cubicle. Inside were a table, two chairs and a padded bed mounted on a hydraulic mechanism. She took a seat and pointed him to the other as she opened a manila folder.

'Right, Mr Budgen,' she said in a business-like manner, glancing at the notes, 'what's the problem?' She waited for the lisp, stutter or minor speech impediment so many body builders seemed to have. To her surprise his voice was normal.

'Well, it's my shoulder. I've got a pain across the top of it – the deltoid, I think.'

She wilted inwardly – treating weights addicts was a nightmare. She prepared herself to be interrogated by him, Gestapo-style. 'OK, do you have any idea what caused it?'

He remembered the last thrust of the tyre iron, and how it had gone clean through the man's skull, jarring on the tarmac below. 'Digging out a tree root. I was sort of hacking down at it with a spade.'

'And this was how long ago?'

'Four days.'

'Right. Did the pain come on suddenly or more gradually, afterwards?'

'Pretty much straight away.'

'Does anything you do on a daily basis aggravate the injury?'

'Well, I'm a van driver. Holding the steering wheel, especially to turn it, doesn't help.'

'OK, could you take your T-shirt off and point out to me exactly where the pain is?' she asked.

He suddenly felt nervous as he pulled the T-shirt over his head. Exposed to her clinical stare, he reached over with his left hand and placed two of his fingers on the top of his shoulder. 'Just in here,' he said, rotating his fingertips in the flesh. She shaded the area in on a sexless outline of a male on the sheet before her.

'What kind of pain is it? Burning? Stabbing? Aching?'

'More of an ache.'

'And on a scale of nought to ten, with ten being the worst pain you could imagine, how would you describe it?'

He didn't like even to admit to pain, let alone measure it. 'Um – about six or seven.'

'Is that better or worse than when you first injured it?'

'A bit better.'

She got up and walked behind him. A trickle of sweat ran down from his armpit. Cupping his right elbow in her palm and placing her other hand on top of his shoulder, she took his upper arm through a range of movements, asking at which point the pain flared up. His entire body was glistening before she said he could put his top back on. As he pulled it over his head she quickly wiped her sweat-covered hands on the backs of her trousers.

'OK, Mr Budgen, you've got a resolving supraspinatus tendonitis.'

'What does that mean?' he asked, looking alarmed.

'You've strained the rotator cuff muscle in your shoulder. It's usually sustained through over-use or suddenly repeating an unusual movement.' She smiled. 'Like digging out a tree root. You just need to rest it, avoid all aggravating movements and keep applying ice to it as often as possible.'

'I go to the gym a lot,' he said, urgently. No kidding, she said to herself. 'When can I start lifting weights again?'

Here we go, she thought. 'Well, it's getting better, but I'd say at least three weeks.'

'Three weeks! What – all exercises or just the shoulder press?'

'Well, legs and torso are OK, of course. But any upper body stuff I wouldn't advise, unless it involves no shoulder movement. Bicep and tricep curls perhaps.'

'Lat pull-downs? Shrugs? Chest press?' He fired off the questions.

'They all involve some shoulder movement. If your shoulder isn't totally healed you'll carry on aggravating it and prolong the injury – especially with the nature of your job.' She paused, but not long enough to let him wrest control from her again. 'Is there anything else you'd like to ask?'

'Yeah,' he said slowly, 'but it's not my shoulder. It's my jaw. It aches like mad, a real throb right in the muscle that bunches out when you clench your teeth.'

'You should really make an appointment with your GP and get another referral for that,' she said, re-ordering the notes in the folder. 'Though I'll tell you now it will be your tempero mandibula joint; where the lower and upper jaws join together. If it turns into a chronic problem it can cause lockjaw which is extremely difficult to treat.' She closed the folder and looked up. 'It's usually stress-related – is there anything making you especially tense at the moment? If you can resolve that, the problem usually sorts itself out.'

He kept his eyes away from the poster of the young girl holding a Ventolin inhaler to her mouth. 'Not apart from the usual money hassles.'

'Well,' she said, showing him back through the curtains, 'if your shoulder worsens, let me know, otherwise I'll discharge you in three weeks. And if you start grinding your jaw at night, definitely see your doctor – he can prescribe a gum-shield to stop you wrecking your teeth. Good luck.'

Chapter 21
The Hunter

He couldn't face telling his mother when he first got home so he went straight up to his room instead. As usual sleep was nowhere near. He flicked on his computer and cancelled the little wizard before he was even halfway through his greeting of 'Last night's full moon won't be repeated for . . .' Moving the cursor straight over to the 'Joy Rider' icon, he double-clicked it to start up the game and played like an automaton for several hours before exhaustion finally won.

When he woke it was early evening. Quietly he crossed to his bedroom door and listened for any sounds downstairs. He couldn't even bear the thought of beginning to tell her. But the house was silent. He went down and found his mother's note on the kitchen table. 'Derek and I have gone to the jazz at the Royal Oak. Didn't want to disturb you. Quiche and cold potatoes in the fridge.' He ate quickly, washed up his plate and went straight back to his room. Later he heard the stairs creaking as they went quietly to bed.

Sunday morning and he couldn't put it off any longer. He got up, showered, dressed and slowly walked down the stairs. His mum and Derek were in the kitchen, the smell of coffee filling the air and papers covering the table.

'My, my – it's alive!' his stepdad joked.

'Morning, love,' said his mum. 'Looks like you've caught up on some sleep. Would you like bacon and eggs?'

'Please.' He sat down.

'Been reading about this Motorway Murderer, Andy,' announced his stepdad, snapping the paper in his hands. 'It must be a great case to be involved in – from an experience point of view. Bloody awful from any other. That was his fourth the other night – and the little girl still hasn't been found.'

His mum piped up from the cooker, 'I've got some good news. Your grandpa phoned last night – I didn't want to disturb you. He's coming up to stay in a few weeks' time and can't wait to hear all about your new job and how you're getting along. Isn't that nice?'

He looked from one beaming face to the other.

'What with the job and visitors – at this rate you'll be wanting your own flat soon, I bet,' said his stepdad.

Andy gulped as the implications of both comments coursed through his mind. Ignoring his stepdad's remark he asked, 'How's Grandpa getting here?' Trying to inject some cheer into his voice.

His mum's face soured a little. 'He's insisting on driving, of course. Doing his usual trick of setting off at eight once the traffic's died down. There's no persuading him otherwise, even after he broke down on the way up here last time. So he'll be arriving at gone midnight – if he isn't delayed.'

Andy struggled to keep a calm exterior.

'So. Are you back on shift this morning?' Derek asked enthusiastically.

Everything hung in the air between them. Obligations and expectations balanced against the humiliating truth. He licked his lips and took a breath in. 'Yes,' he replied. 'I'm on an eight till six.'

'Well, all your shirts are ironed,' his mum immediately replied.

He chewed on his breakfast with a dry mouth, idly flicking through the magazine at his elbow. After a while he forced the last lump down and reluctantly looked at the clock on the wall. 'I'd better be off then,' he announced. 'See you tonight.'

'Good luck,' they both said simultaneously.

He threw his kit bag in the boot of his mum's old blue Volvo 340

GL and set off, not knowing where to go. He followed the road in a daze, drifted out of the suburbs and into the city centre. 'Parking – free on Sundays.' The sign caught his eye and he pulled up in the empty lot. Leaving his car, he walked slowly towards the precinct.

He found the atmosphere strange, as if a daytime curfew was in operation. The streets were deserted, everyone cocooned inside, feeling the first crawling approach of Monday morning. All the shops were closed, shutters pulled down, turning the normally colourful street into a succession of grey screens. Only the graffiti artists had utilised the advertising space for signing their spiky names. He walked through the pub district, looking at the leftovers from the previous night's activity all around. Fractured and broken glasses, crumpled cans, handfuls of dropped chips. The bins over-flowed with rubbish – polystyrene hamburger containers, grease-proof paper pressed into balls, bottles and crisp packets. Cow-pats of vomit in shop doorways. Outside a kebab shop shrunken shreds of lettuce and cabbage lay strewn across the pavement. Pigeons flapped away from where they'd been pecking at the remains of a chicken carcass, the struts of its ribcage preventing the bones from falling through the gaps of the drain cover it had been thrown on to. Next came the spattered drops of dried blood, flurries of it leading to rusty hand prints where the person had finally fallen.

He could almost hear the blundering carnival of just a few hours ago. People chatting, smiling, hugging, laughing, shrieking, whooping, kissing, giggling, squeezing, slurring, stumbling, spin-ning, pushing, shoving, snarling, shouting, punching, kicking, running, puking, collapsing.

He sat down on some steps and, noticing the bright squares of card scattered all around him, gathered a few together.

'Revelation at the Shebeen. £6 before 10 p.m. with this flyer.'

'Excess at Cartagena. £5 & free drink before midnite with this flyer.'

'Eden at the Promise. Drinks promos all night. £2 off entry with this flyer.'

'Full Moon Wobbler at Trifle. £5 Fri & Sat plus a free drink both nights with this flyer.'

He looked at the jelly-like words spelling 'Full Moon' and somewhere, deep in his mind, a connection was made between the date he'd seen the broken-down car and his sighting of the freak a couple of nights before. It lay there pulsating, waiting to be discovered, but the neon colours and 3D shadows – with their promise of escape and oblivion – distracted him. He stared at the cards as if they were communications from another world. As if some UFO had swooped there before dawn, dropping them in its wake. So many nights spent in a silent car, witness to nothing.

A bin lorry trundled around the corner, flashing lights hardly visible now it was day. He shoved the flyers into his pocket, got quickly to his feet and resumed his lonely wandering.

Chapter 22
The Searcher

More flies were emerging from somewhere. They crawled over each other's backs at the base of his windows, swarming on the sills. He went through the house again, turning up the threadbare carpets, checking beneath his fridge and at the back of his kitchen cupboards. But he couldn't find where they were coming from.

So he sat on the chair in his kitchen, palms resting on the table in front of him, and stared at the shelves of Perspex boxes spanning the opposite wall. As the bars of sunlight slid slowly from one box to the next he endlessly replayed all of his forages in his head, searching for clues or hints. Where were they watching him from? How were they following him?

His mind's eye turned to the yellowed netting in his neighbours' windows and he considered the silent phone lines that stretched like the first strands of a spider's web to the poles in the street. He knew there was one in next-door's house because he sometimes heard its shrill ring through the wall. What information passed along those lines? Where did the wires lead to?

He'd read about small devices that could be placed inside a car; they allowed a vehicle to be shadowed over large distances. He'd read about even smaller ones too. Ones that could be placed inside a person. Uneasily he raised a hand towards his face and the blue-bottle that had been trying to feed at the tear duct of his left eye launched itself out into the still expanse of the room. With his fingers he probed the skin at the back of his neck, feeling for any tell-tale lumps. He located a nodule at the top of his spine and his breath caught in his throat. But then a childhood memory returned and he realised it had been there for years.

Next day, and the soft sigh of the fridge door opening broke the silence of the kitchen. A few flies responded to the noise by adding the irritating buzz of their wings. The low drone reminded him of the noise the motorway made: he missed the grassy seclusion it offered. Light from the little bulb inside bounced off the empty white interior. He needed milk, yoghurt, vegetables, things like that. It meant going out, and his wrist was too painful for driving. He peered round the side of the window blinds – it wasn't too busy. Most people would be at work by now, and the strollers on the street would have silver hair and grey clothes. Generally they didn't bother him, perhaps the odd 'morning' whispered from elderly lips.

He locked the door behind him and set off towards the super-market. Wires hung in the air above him, stretching along the street as he paced cautiously below. At the corner he checked both ways, searching for kerb-crawling cars or anyone loitering in the street. Nothing. He pressed on, leaving the residential streets and entering an area scattered with shops. Blanked-out glass of betting offices, grilled and padlocked off-licences and others whose windows had just been replaced by chipboard. Posters behind another dusty window read 'Closing down sale. Everything under £2', but the inside was bare except for a pile of letters on the doormat. He reached the noisier main street, the procession of cars more constant, the pavement interspersed with pedestrians. Not far until he reached the low wall of the supermarket car park. He lowered his head and willed himself forward. Reaching the corner of a side street he was forced to stop to allow a car to pull out. Glancing over its roof he saw a middle-aged woman standing on the other side. She met his eyes and he looked down. The car eased into the main road and he watched her ankles to see which side of her he should pass on. But her feet didn't move. He stepped across the narrow road and a voice barred his way.

'Excuse me, sir, I noticed you're walking to your destination.'

He half glanced up, and to his horror saw the person was stepping backwards, trying to address him. A red clipboard held to the side prevented him from passing.

'It really will take just a couple of minutes. We're collecting data on behalf of the local council about the use of public transport in the area. Could you spare me a moment?'

He'd always assumed that it would be men who came for him. Confused, he couldn't think of a single thing to say.

'Thank you. Could I take your postcode, please?'

So they were trying to find out exactly where he lived. He started blinking rapidly as the pavement lurched and then began to undulate beneath his feet.

'Are you all right, sir?'

From the corner of his eye he saw an open doorway, the dim interior punctuated by softly coloured lights. He took a step backwards and his heel scraped down the shin of a person closing in from behind. Whoever it was let out a pained cry and he jumped with both feet across the pavement and fell into the dark interior.

The sudden change in light left him squinting and a voice by his side buzzed, 'Come and try it, punk.' He turned and saw cacti caught in the mirrors of the American policeman's sunglasses. Bells started to ring, and sensing space to his right, he moved into it with one steadying hand on the cool and sloping surfaces of the machines that lined the wall. Coloured lights surged behind the clear plastic fronts, columns climbing higher and higher until they touched panels which excitedly began to flash. No one had followed him inside and he stepped hesitantly towards the corner of the room. Halfway along the next wall a youngish man slouched in a brightly lit booth, reading a paper. He turned to the machine directly in front. A market stall display of garish fruit lay before him, each line labelled with increasing amounts of money.

As his eyes adjusted to the dim light, he looked around properly. Further along the row stood an old woman. The rapidly blinking lights had hypnotised her, and like a robot she raised an arm to press money into the top of the machine. It responded with a flicker, a tune and a spin of its dials. The row of fat buttons beneath her sagging front glowed red and she stabbed at a couple before reverently pressing the green one at the end. The dials spun again and a couple of coins clunk-clicked into the tray. At the top of the room a man bent over a pool table. The long light suspended above it shone down, making the spot of metal in his ear glitter. In the shadows behind sat another person, his cue resting in the crook of his crossed leg. From the side of the room behind him he heard the strained whine of an engine racing. The noise came from a mock car, complete with steering wheel, bucket seat, rear lights and registration. In front of the car was a large screen showing wildly veering footage of a parched country road.

He realised the man in the booth was staring at him. Needing time to think, he scraped the coins for the supermarket from his pocket and copied the old woman. The images of fruit blurred on the little cylinders, before each came to a stop and the lights went out. To bring the machine back to life he fed more money in, pressing the green button and watching the miniature light show.

After a while he'd used up all his coins, so tentatively he walked back to the patch of brightness that spilled across the giant door-mat. He peered out and saw the woman was still there, clipboard held before her. As he watched she tried to stop someone else, repeating the question she had used to him. The person skirted around her, apologetically tapping his watch with a forefinger to indicate his hurry.

He couldn't risk her catching him again, so went over to the racing car machine. A young man was now crouched in the low-slung seat, angrily slamming the automatic gear stick back and forth, harshly stamping on the pedals. At times his car skidded dangerously close to the crowds at the edge of the screen, even spraying them with clouds of dust and grit. As the landscape scrolled back and forth he caught the odd glimpse of sparkling blue sea between the arid hills. After a few minutes a man appeared at the other side of the machine. He looked down at the player and his eyebrows lifted in recognition. In the distance a banner appeared and as the car raced towards it, the letters grew larger before eventually reading 'Finish'. The car passed under it, the revs dropped and it crunched to a halt. 'Stage 1 complete. Congratulations – today's best time' was superimposed across the screen.

'Not lost your touch on that course then,' the other spectator casually remarked.

The man in the bucket seat looked up quickly.

'Have you just come off shift then?'

The driver looked back at the screen. 'Er . . . yes,' he replied, tilting his head awkwardly backwards.

As usual he was at the edge of a conversation that didn't include him. He quietly moved across the thick carpet back to the doorway. The woman outside was busy questioning an elderly couple. He began to edge out of the left-hand side of the door to head for the supermarket but checked his step, realising that he'd pushed all his money into the machine. So instead he switched to the right-hand side, slipping past the woman and heading home, empty-handed.

Chapter 23
The Killer

'Fishies!' his wife said. Inside the aquarium, slithers of neon darted between the plastic fronds. His daughter strained forward in her mother's arms, trying to press her face against the thick, warm glass. His attention returned to the large hardback book held in his hands. Images of Roman legionnaires filled the pages before him. Clad in padded leather breastplates and brandishing squat, ugly swords they marched forward in an impenetrable line. He turned another couple of pages to the section on gladiators. There in the sandy-floored arena two fighters squared up to each other. One wore a helmet, armour, and held a trident. In his other hand he whirled a net above his head. The man facing him seemed almost naked in comparison. Wearing only a loincloth, he held out a small shield and thin sword. Though the illustrations were childishly simplistic, Dave examined them with a medical concern, scrutinising every aspect of their physiques. He compared their bodies to his own – though they lacked modern-day knowledge of weight training, these men had had all day, every day, to train for their art. He wondered what sort of diet they'd had. Cheese, eggs, milk, chicken – probably not too different from his own except for the high-protein powders and occasional injections he had access to.

'Dave, you're meant to be choosing books for Jasmine – that's the kids' section,' his wife called over.

He grunted and shoved the book back into the nearest space, then moved on to the babies' corner. He looked with dismay at the untidy pile. It appeared as if the books had been poured into the great big box. Rummaging around, he selected a few on the basis of how new they looked, and nothing else. 'These'll do,' he said, crossing over to his wife and daughter.

'We had that one the other week,' she said, nodding at the top one.

'She won't remember that,' he answered. 'Anyway the rest are all scummy and ripped. Come on – let's get out of here.' He looked through the aquarium, into the main hall on the other side. A few distorted, wavery forms sat reading at the rows of tables.

'OK,' his wife replied, standing up and plonking Jasmine into the buggy. Immediately the child began to moan, pointing a finger at the glass. 'We'll see the fishies another time,' she consoled, then added, 'Do you want to go to the park?' The word 'park' caused the little girl to look expectantly around. 'Right, let's get these stamped.'

Outside the main doors they paused at the fork in the road, Dave making for the footbridge. 'Can't we use the underpass – it makes me nervous pushing her across that thing,' she said.

'Whatever,' he replied, and directed the buggy down the curving path and into the tunnel. As they walked its narrow length the plastic clattering of the buggy's wheels bounced back at them from the graffiti-covered walls. At the other end they took a couple of turns along quiet rows of houses, emerging at the small square of grass with its tiny playground. The rounded poles of a climbing frame jutted out from an asphalt square and, as usual, Dave looked at it, remembering how the cold metal of the frame in his old park used to numb his hands when he was younger.

They reached the waist-high wooden fence that closed in the children's play area and Dave used the front wheels of the buggy to push the swing gate open. The notice nailed to the front read, 'No dogs. This play area is for children under 7 only.' But as they passed the Wendy house he could see the empty cider cans and cigarette butts littering the mulch floor of the little room. Warily he scanned the ground for dog shit. They stopped at the only adult-sized object inside: a gouged and lacerated wooden bench. He sat down heavily and watched as his wife lifted Jasmine from the buggy and carried her towards the bucket seat swings. As she caught sight of them her little legs began to kick.

On the other side of the low fence a few pigeons jostled around an object in the grass, urgently pecking at it. Every so often one succeeded in removing a larger piece – then, with a shake of its head, would attempt to break the fragment down further. Usually the entire morsel flicked out of its beak and another bird immediately fell upon it. He watched the process, wondering what it could be they were so eagerly feeding on. Eventually curiosity got the better of him and he stood up – then wished he hadn't as he realised it was a dried-out piece of dog turd. He sat back down and watched a slightly older kid clambering the wrong way up the slide. The enclosure gate creaked open and his little sister ran in. Immediately he turned away and tried to shut out the sound of her excited voice. A few moments later Sally came walking over and placed Jasmine back in the buggy. She then delved around in the compartment under the seat, handed a biscuit to the little girl and sat down next to Dave with the pile of library books.

'Oh, she loves these ones – with the little family of talking peas.' She began turning the pages and Dave, not wanting to look over to where the children's voices were coming from, took another book from her lap. An idyllic farmyard scene, with doe-eyed cows chatting to rosy-jowled pigs. The little girl began to screech with delight and from the periphery of his vision he could see the boy stalking around the Wendy house. She ran inside and he crouched below the side window and said, 'I'm the big bad wolf and I'll huff and I'll puff and I'll blow your house down!' She started to squeal. Slowly the boy lifted his head towards the window. Dave's temples began to throb and he stared intently at the page. A flutter of wings by the buggy and he glanced to his left. A pigeon was pacing towards the biscuit his daughter had dropped.

He jumped to his feet, slapping his hand against the book and shouting, 'Piss off!'

Startled, it took flight and his daughter began to cry at the sudden commotion.

'Dave, you great idiot,' complained his wife, getting to her feet. The two kids were looking at him in silence.

'They're bloody vermin, those things. Carry all sorts of diseases.'

'You didn't need to shout like that,' she replied, placing the books back into the buggy. 'Come on, Jasmine, it's time for your lunch.' She set off without waiting for him and he followed awkwardly behind, avoiding the two children's silent stares.

On the other side of the park the rows of houses were smaller and thinner-looking; most with satellite dishes sprouting like toadstools from beneath the gutters. Theirs was now just a few streets away. They reached the main road that ran along the other side of the park and stopped. Used as a rat run to avoid the traffic lights of the main street nearby, their progress across it was halted by the moving barrier of cars. Sally looked expectantly in both directions, waiting for a gap in the traffic. Beside her, Dave's headache got worse as he began to clench and unclench his jaw.

'Not one of these bastards is going to let us cross,' he commented bitterly.

'We could always walk to the pelican crossing just down there,' his wife replied flatly.

His anger mounted as each driver, eager to make their short cut count, shot past with eyes fixed rigidly on the car in front. Abruptly he stepped into the road, holding up one hand. The approaching driver lurched to a stop, an incredulous look on his face. 'Come on, we can cross now,' he ordered his wife.

'Jesus Christ, Dave,' she said.

'Come on!' he repeated more loudly, stepping across the white line in the middle of the road and forcing the traffic on the other side to a halt. The lead driver held his hand up and was about to press on the car horn, but when he saw the expression on Dave's face he altered the gesture and waved them across. Dave strode over, his wife waving embarrassed thank-yous in his wake.

Back at the flat he switched the telly on and slumped on to the sofa. Jasmine was placed on the rug and the pushchair was folded up. He idly turned the pages of the paper he'd slipped from the library, stopping to survey a full-page car ad. The photograph was of a stretch of motorway, empty except for the gleaming vehicle and the headline 'Advance yourself'. Dave shook his head at the surreal nature of the scene and turned the page to a mass of loan company adverts offering car finance deals. Beyond the paper the TV programme cut to commercials, and soothing classical music started up as a driver, safely ensconced in the calm interior of his car, swept along an empty road. He flicked on some sort of cruise control, settling contentedly back in his seat as a pair of ghostly hands, no doubt symbolising the spirit of the car itself, began to massage his neck and shoulders. Dave turned the TV off, folded the paper and closed his eyes. Shut out the absurdity of it all.

Chapter 24
The Hunter

He set off into the early-morning traffic, relieved to be clear of the house before they were up. At the train station he parked his car in the staff area, telling the attendant he was transport police, reporting for duty. He picked his bag out of the boot and walked back through the gates. Another day to use up. At the side of the building he approached a door leading into the main station area. As soon as it slid back a seething mass of activity was revealed. Office workers walking quickly past each other, briefcases and bags clutched at their sides. He observed them, wrapped up in their petty work-place concerns, completely oblivious of what only he knew. He resented their ignorance.

He slipped inside the door and was instantly carried along by the current of people. Seeing he was being swept towards the main exit, he struggled against the tide, getting the back of his knees clipped by a briefcase before making it to the entrance on to the platforms. The space above him dramatically increased and he raised his eyes to the arching framework of glass panels and metal struts. A diesel engine revved, sending a rolling billow of blue smoke towards the high roof. Screens hung from metal arms, listing times and destinations in flickering columns.

Aware that he was still in the way of the crowd, he moved to the side and found a gap from which he could watch the trains arrive.

Way up the track, beyond the huge roof's protective covering, one approached. It eased to a whining stop in front of the heavy buffers at the track's end. The doors suddenly gaped and it vomited its contents on to the platform. The lumpy cloth-covered mass turned and immediately began flowing towards him. He watched impassively as it reached the dam of the ticket barriers where it was held, pooling out backwards, seeping through gradually to merge with the flood beyond.

Punctuated by regular announcements from the Tannoy system, the morning wore on. As it did, the trains lessened in frequency and their contents subsided to a trickle. Eventually he left his position and walked out on to the station concourse. Black cab engines idled in a line to his left. Looking down the sloping road that led to one of the city's main streets, he noticed the thin white jet wash of an aeroplane stretching across the grey sky. About halfway across, a narrow crane, its arm almost vertical, rose above the rooftops, tip straining just high enough to touch the plane's trail. For an instant he had the impression it was an enormous clothes prop and the plane trail an immense clothesline spanning one side of the city to the other. All the dirty washing, he thought, is on the streets around me. Involuntarily he shuddered and set off down the road.

Up ahead a doorway fisherman plied his trade, rocking on the balls of his feet, casting into the passing crowd, trying to hook his glance into someone's eyes. Andy looked just a little too long and, bam! The man struck. Quickly he reeled himself in on his invisible line right up to Andy's side and began his patter.

'Sorry to bother you, mate, it's just I'm in a spot of bother . . .'

'Sorry,' said Andy, shaking his head.

The man carried on regardless, urgently reciting his lines. 'I just need a couple of quid – someone's nicked my wallet, you see, and I've got to get home because my wee kid is . . .'

'Sorry,' Andy repeated without breaking his step.

The man stuck with him, but knowing Andy hadn't really bitten was already scanning the faces of approaching people. 'I'd never normally ask, but it's just that . . .' Abruptly he broke off and weaved his way through the flow to the other side of the pavement. 'Excuse me. Sorry to bother you, mate.' The next line was lost in the sound of footsteps.

He spent the rest of the day browsing through shops. At lunch-time he bought a paper and killed a couple of hours in a café by reading the news from cover to cover. He consumed the reports on the Motorway Murderer more eagerly than his food. The police still had no witnesses or useful evidence to announce – it seemed they hadn't even figured out that the last one up near Carlisle was either unrelated or a copy-cat killing. The editorial comment had quoted a police source as saying that suspicions were now firmly on someone imitating a breakdown recovery vehicle of some sort – perhaps a motorbike. The paper went on to report that the various motorway maintenance departments dotted around the country employed at least 3,800 workers, many on a seasonal basis. Alto-gether they estimated there were more than 6,000 vehicles authorised to stop on the hard shoulder. More worryingly, it reported gleefully, one of their undercover reporters had success-fully made it into a depot and obtained the keys to a van, complete with markings and roof-mounted flashing lights. While acknow-ledging the dangers of staying inside a broken-down car, the paper advised it was still a better option than waiting outside your vehicle. It stressed the importance of keeping doors locked and asking for ID before even lowering a window.

Andy dismissed the conjecture – they could prattle on all they wanted about fake breakdown vehicles, only he knew what had been lurking on that stretch of the M40. He wandered to a nearby square and found an empty bench, away from the bunch of middle-aged men clutching big plastic bottles of cider. From each corner, newspaper sellers shouted the early-evening headlines. Daylight began to dim and the square grew busier as more and more people emerged from office buildings into the late-afternoon light. They marched quickly past, heads bowed, bent on getting home as soon as possible. Soon the numbers had swelled so that no one could maintain a straight line, everyone had to adjust and swerve past all the others doing exactly the same thing.

From ledges high above, the various flocks of starlings that had sat perched all afternoon decided, with one mind, that it was time to return to their roosts for the night. In an instant, scores of birds launched themselves into space with a barrage of little wing beats. Flecks of droppings rained down as they swooped and circled each other, chattering furiously, waiting for the sign that would draw them off in a perfectly synchronised display. In the square below Andy watched many faces flash annoyed glances up at the stupid animals who decided, with dumb regularity, to fly off home at exactly the same time each day.

As evening closed in the square slowly emptied. An older man sat down at the other end of the bench and glanced towards him. Andy could feel his lingering gaze. He got up, crossed the square and began walking across the city. After a good twenty minutes the shop front he was looking for appeared, the red velvet backdrop behind the windows showing off the display of china teddy bears and vases mounted on plastic plinths. This was where he and a few others would spend their breaks from the supermarket round the corner. He stepped into the dark interior and went straight to the racing car game on the left-hand side of the room. He fished out all the change in his pocket and climbed inside. Then, looking at the pile of money in his palm, he picked out the pound coins and inserted them one after another into the slot. The machine beeped and his credit built up. Once all his money was in he flicked through the rally venues, settling on the stony tracks of Cyprus.

The lights changed from red to green and he was off, instantly absorbed by the twisting course. Whenever the voice warned him of a sharp turn he would switch pedals, touching the brakes and pulling the gear stick back a notch. Once round, the stick was shoved away and the accelerator jammed back to the floor. He drove with a manic urgency before coming to the end of the first leg, and as he crossed the line his engine died. Breathing deeply, he flexed his fingers as the outline of the next stage flashed up.

'Not lost your touch on that course then.' The voice came from just behind his right shoulder. He looked up, and to his dismay saw one of the people he used to work with at the supermarket smiling down. Reality flooded back. 'Have you just come off shift then?' he continued.

Andy looked back towards the screen and was aware of another, slightly built man, melting away behind his left shoulder.

'Er . . . yes,' he replied. He couldn't sit with his head craned back like this and hold a conversation. Reluctantly he pressed the pause button and climbed out. 'Yeah, I've just finished a huge day shift. Always need to let off steam after one of them. So how are you, John?'

The person nodded. 'OK, thanks. How are you finding the police?'

The mention of police caused the two pool players to look over and their conversation dropped to a whisper.

'It's excellent,' replied Andy, uneasily looking to his side, but the other man had disappeared.

'So what brings you here then? I thought you couldn't wait to get away,' said John with an ironic smile.

'No, no,' said Andy, playing for time. 'I still like to pop in – play on this.' He patted the machine, as he would a prized car. 'It's really good for your driving reflexes. Better than the simulator at the station,' he added weakly.

'Yeah?' said John, looking at the machine with renewed interest, then back at Andy, forcing him to carry on.

'Definitely. I'm taking my advanced driving test soon – been in a few chases already.' But he didn't want to talk about the job, didn't want to make any more up. 'So what's been happening back at the supermarket?'

'Not much,' replied John, instantly sounding bored. 'They've still got me pottering around at the back. Sorting stock out. Sometimes I do a bit of shelf stacking, you know – if I'm on a night shift. Remember that bloke called Waite?' Andy nodded. 'He got sacked for nicking Gillette razors. Sixty quid's worth they found in his bag.' He paused, as if remembering something he'd forgotten. 'They might be shutting this one though and opening a superstore out near the dual carriageway. Said all our jobs will be safe, but we still have to reapply.' He looked at the machine again. 'So you reckon this thing helps with your driving? Tell you what, you've done well, Andy. Getting out of it and becoming a thief taker and all that.' Andy could sense the question coming, but couldn't escape before it did. 'Could you get me an application form? If I practised enough on this thing, do you think I could get in?'

Andy blustered, 'Well, I don't know. I mean, you've just missed the application date for this six months.' The deception was exhausting him. 'I got the application address from the library, can't remember where it was written.' He couldn't face asking John if he had any GCSEs – he suspected he hadn't. But already the idea of sourcing an application form himself seemed to have dented his enthusiasm. 'Look, I've got to go, paperwork and all that.' He looked at the machine, with all its credit left. 'Finish off my round for me if you want.'

'Ah, cheers, Andy. I'll see you around then.'

'Yeah, see you around. And good luck if you apply.'

As he walked out of the arcade the pinball machine by the door called out, 'Hasta la vista baby! Ha! Ha! Ha!'

Coming back through his front door, he actually trod on the letter lying on the doormat. 'Mum?' he called out, but the house was empty. They must have set off for the day before the post had arrived. He ripped open the envelope and sat down at the kitchen table to read the letter.

Seeing that it was from the Divisional Department of Personnel, he skimmed over it as fast as he could, eager to discover what it had to say.

'. . . hope this time has given you the opportunity to recuperate . . . sick leave is due to conclude next Monday . . . initially you will carry out administrative and other duties . . . 5.45 p.m. on Monday is your first appointment . . . until the counsellor approves you as fit . . . cannot allow you to resume active patrol work . . . please report to Supervisor Reynolds in the control room at 8.00 a.m. . . . Final note, Inspector Marsh has stated that you are to avoid all contact with Sergeant Walker . . . instruction to be strictly adhered to . . .'

So that was it, he was confined to desk work, not trusted to be in a patrol car. Booked in with a shrink. He folded the letter up as small as it would go and hid it at the back of his wallet.

Chapter 25
The Searcher

As the days passed and no one came banging on his door he'd begun to hope that they didn't know exactly where he lived. Fear and apprehension gradually waned in the security of his home and resentment began to stir. Why must they prevent him from getting to the land that was his own? Why? Hunger lolled in his stomach, insisting that he do something. The last of his tins had been finished the day before and he grudgingly accepted that he'd have to go out.

The bruise had spread under the skin of his wrist, creeping down on to the back of his hand like a stain. With driving still too painful he would have to try and walk to the supermarket again. Upstairs he stood at the crack in the draped sheeting and angled first his right eye, then his left, to the gap – checking up and down the street, waiting for it to be completely deserted before setting off. Finally everything was still and he rushed down the stairs, fumbling for his key. Once outside he stuck to the side streets, unsure who might be watching or following. Finally he reached the car park, unhitched a trolley from the stack and pushed it through the doors.

Humming rows of freezers and brilliant light instantly set his nerves on edge as his trolley trilled over the tiled floor. Other shoppers shuffled along between the freezers, browsing with heads lowered like cows in a meadow. Beyond lay shelves packed to the edge with shining tins, bottles and jars. Rows of parallel aisles stretching far away. He entered one and the shelves reared to head height on each side of him, leaning in and forcing him onwards. To justify his visit he nervously placed a couple of tins on to the wire base of the trolley. They began a tiny clanking noise as he started forward again. Pointless music trickled from invisible speakers around him, and glancing up he saw the lens of a camera possibly tracking him. He placed more cans in the trolley.

To distract his mind from the mounting feeling of dread, he imagined he was driving a car as he approached a corner. Changing gears, he took it a little shakily and the cans clinked louder. More aisles loomed up. Turning was impossible so he carried on as the cheese wire between his temples drew tighter. He threw in a couple of packets of something, knowing that he had to hurry up. Braking at a crossroads, he checked over his shoulder and dragged the trolley round, changed back up and accelerated away. Boxes of stuff glided past his head and into the periphery of his tunnel vision. The air, pumped from dusty vents above, smelled of cardboard. As his anxiety grew, he moved up into fourth, looking for a point where he could at least see the exit. His breathing accelerated as he shot along, foot now fully down in desperation. He reached the end-of-aisle and attempted to swing his trolley across, but he was going too fast, its arc was too wide. The front corner smashed into an end-of-aisle promotional display of jam, crunching several jars on impact. The cardboard shelf unit started to topple and his trolley, jarred by the jars, abruptly stopped. His momentum took him on, so his knee caught on its handle bar and he sprawled over the top. He landed amongst a cascading crash, red jelly squirting all around him. He staggered to his feet, globules and shards dripping off him, trolley on its side.

Abandoning it, he ran for the tills, hurdling the chain between two closed ones. A shout came from behind and he was out of the doors, sprinting across the car park. Footsteps behind him. He veered round a corner on to a long side street – the next turn was a couple of hundred yards ahead. He could feel his heart beating erratically, short bursts followed by great big stuttering thumps.

The footsteps behind were getting closer. He looked down at his knees and willed them to pump faster. But his breath wouldn't come and he came to a grinding halt, pressing his cheek against the wall, palms flat against the bricks, willing the mortar to absorb him as he waited for the grabbing hands.

When nothing happened he opened his eyes and looked to his side. The street behind was empty.

Chapter 26
The Killer

When the phone reached its fifth ring he twisted his upper body round on the sofa and shouted through the door, 'Get that, will you, Sal – it's bound to be your mum.'

He heard the washing-up brush clatter on to the draining board. 'Please, don't strain your fat arse,' his wife said as she passed the open doorway on her way to where the phone sat in the narrow hallway. He kept his eyes fixed on the TV screen. 'Oh, hi, Bernard. Yeah, he's here,' he just heard over the commentary. From behind, two hands descended in front of his face. One held the phone, the other covered the mouthpiece. 'It's bound to be your mum,' his wife whispered into his ear, tongue pushed behind her lower lip in imitation of an idiot.

'Fuck off,' he retorted and snatched the phone from her grasp. 'Dave here,' he said.

'Hi, Dave, Bernard Clarke speaking.'

'All right, mate.'

'Yeah, fine.' He sounded stressed. 'Listen – I've got an urgent one to Hull. Batch of solenoids and some other stuff, needed for early morning. Can you do it? It's a big favour, mate.'

He allowed a second's pause before saying, 'No problem. Straight away?'

''Fraid so – the boxes will be in the docking bay. Cheers, Dave, you're a star.'

'OK.' He pressed the hang-up button and pushed the antenna back into the handset. 'Sal – I've got a delivery. It's gonna be most of the night.'

'OK, hon – I'll see you when you get in. And drive carefully!' she called as he grabbed his keys off the hook by the door.

Five minutes later he was driving his van out of the mess in his lock-up. He jumped from the vehicle, and keeping his eyes away from the wardrobe, swung the lock-up door down and padlocked it shut.

Fifteen minutes later he was waving hello to the night watchman and driving round the back of the plant to the deserted docking area. He parked and strode over to the despatches office at the side. Inside stacks of boxes crowded what little floor space was left. 'Delivery of solenoids over to Hull?' he asked the bloke at the far end, whilst examining the dockets on the top of the piles nearest him.

'The ones just to your right, mate. There's directions in there too. Apparently it's a big place – you can't miss it.'

After piling the boxes into the side of his van Dave checked there was still no one else in the loading bay then stepped over to the side where a load of plain grey boiler suits hung from pegs like a row of discarded skins. Quickly he selected an XXL size and threw it into the back of the van.

For once the place really was easy to find – floodlights lit up the corrugated white sides from miles off. He pulled up at the security gate and signed in. 'Side building over there,' pointed the security guard.

'Cheers, pal.'

He drove over, parked and carried the boxes to the door. A gaunt little man appeared, eyes beady in his bony head. 'Bring 'em in, bring 'em in,' he said and disappeared back inside. Dave dumped the boxes just inside the door and pulled the docket out of the plastic envelope taped to the top box.

'Right, can't do much with them until the early-morning shift comes on,' said the man, his skin waxy and pale under the strip light. Too many night shifts, thought Dave. 'Fancy a quick brew?'

he continued, turning the kettle on and a portable TV down.

'Yeah, I will, cheers,' said Dave, taking a seat.

The man cleared a space for the mugs and took the other seat. 'I bet you keep your engine in good nick, driving around the motorways at this time,' he commented, scrawling a signature on the docket and tearing off the top sheet.

'Um?' replied Dave.

'You know – with that psycho out there somewhere.'

Dave smiled. 'Let's just say I go prepared.'

'I bet you do,' the man said. 'The way I see it, it's all about survival of the fittest.'

'You what?' answered Dave.

'Well,' he went on and nodded at the TV, eyes shining, 'I was watching one of those David Attenborough programmes the other night, and it's always the knackered-out deer that attracts the tiger. It's the same on the motorway. Once you pull up on that hard shoulder you're separated from the pack, aren't you? Same way tigers go for the injured and lame ones, your psycho goes for people who've broken down. You've got to stay with the herd – it's a survival thing, pure and simple.'

Dave wondered what to say and the echo of a sentence rang in his head. 'That's a bit harsh, mate.'

'Oh, I know,' the man said, pleased at having aired his theory. 'But life is harsh, isn't it, mmm? We might not have a jungle in this country but we've got our bloody motorways!' Laughter rocked him in his seat. 'Hey? Got our bloody motorways!' he repeated triumphantly.

Dave couldn't help chuckling as well. He liked the theory – him as a predator, picking out the ignorant and useless. The ones who couldn't keep up, who hindered the rest by causing traffic jams and other delays. They sat in silence for a while, watching the silent screen and sipping their drinks.

'Well, cheers for the brew, I'd better be on my way,' he eventually said, gulping down the last of his tea.

The man took the empty cup. 'Righty-ho.' He crossed to the sink, absorbed in some other train of thought.

'See you about,' added Dave, pushing open the door.

'Maybe,' answered the man, suddenly adding, 'as long as you beware that tiger!'

As Dave walked to his van he could hear the other man laughing to himself inside.

Heading back through the outskirts of the city he passed a council yard in which a dozen or so cherry pickers were parked. With their crane-like necks, designed for repairing street lights, they jostled together inside the fence like a herd of nervous giraffes. Don't worry, he silently told them, the tiger's not hunting tonight.

Chapter 27
The Hunter

He stopped his car down the street from the security booth at the entrance to the police car park and observed the building. As 8 a.m. approached various police vehicles and civilian cars began to arrive. The cars parked and the drivers collected their bits and pieces and disappeared into the building. As the minutes ticked by the process began to be reversed as the officers coming off shift started heading home. Restarting his engine, he felt a pang of resentment that the cycle had carried on like clockwork without him.

Once inside the building his sense of anonymity increased – people walked past him, totally unaware this was his first day back. He took comfort from the lack of attention as he slipped into the locker room. A few officers finishing their shifts glanced at him. One said, 'Morning.'

Andy nodded back. Despite the assortment of jackets and coats they wore, the white shirts, pressed black trousers and shiny black shoes gave their profession away. He walked up to his locker and, as he searched for the key in his pocket, noticed a corner of paper poking out from one of the ventilation slits at the top of the door. He pulled the page out and looked at the photograph. It had been torn from some sort of war-game magazine and was of a young man clad in battle dress, face smeared with camouflage cream. Paranoia prickled at his ears and he looked to his left and right. No one was paying him any attention. When he wondered who was responsible the face of only one person appeared in his mind.

Five minutes later he stood outside the soundproofed door of the control room. He reached up to knock on it, but just before his knuckles made contact, the door was pulled open from inside and his curled fingers rapped at thin air. Someone hurried past and Andy held the door open, looking into the dimly lit room.

An enormous road map of the area covered the whole of one wall. At regular intervals along the blue lines of motorway were small orange squares, each one marked with the number of the SOS phone located there. Andy looked more closely and saw that the roads were studded with small red light bulbs. Banks of TV screens were mounted on the walls flanking the maps, each one showing footage from various sections of the motorway system. As he watched, some of the screens flicked on to other views, but the flow of traffic always seemed to be constant.

'Constable Seer?'

Andy looked down at the woman in front of him. She was small, overweight and dressed in civilian clothes. He was reminded of his mother. 'I'm Mary Reynolds, the Support Staff Supervisor.'

He wasn't sure how to address her, and felt even more awkward when she held out her hand.

'So, I have the benefit of your assistance for a while,' she continued. 'I'll get you helping with calls from ETBs first, and you can move on to helping the radio operators later.'

Andy looked with dismay at the row of desks and the monitors covering them. Six women, all wearing headsets, sat in front of the screens. 'Now, I'll put you with Alice this morning. She can talk you through the procedure for taking calls from broken-down vehicles. With schools on holiday it should be a nice quiet morning.'

They stopped behind a thin woman of about forty. As Mary placed a hand on her shoulder she looked round, then took her headset off.

'Alice, this is Andrew – or is it Andy?'

'Either will do,' he replied.

'Right. He'll be helping us out for a while.'

They nodded at each other.

'If he can sit with you to begin with, then you can familiarise him with the procedure for taking calls from ETBs.' She looked at Andy. 'That's Emergency Telephone Boxes. Here you go, have this seat.'

She rolled a chair across the carpet to him. 'I'll be round and about.' She smiled and walked away. Alice looked rather uncertainly at him, while some of the other women glanced in his direction.

'Right, Andrew, sit down and I'll tell you how everything works.' Her voice was coarse. As soon as he sat down, he smelt cigarette smoke on her clothes. 'Put on those ear-phones and you can listen in when I get a call.'

Alice slipped her headset back on and Andy did the same.

'OK, the screen is a set one with mandatory questions. When a driver calls us from the motorway, the box he's using lights up on the map. If the phone is located on a stretch where we've got CCTV, we can zoom in on that part of the motorway too. But I'll explain that later. This screen,' she pointed a bright pink fingernail at her right-hand monitor, 'has all the questions we ask. They help to pinpoint the problem as fast as possible. You just start at the top and select the "Yes" or "No" boxes.'

Andy nodded and looked at the first question. It read: 'Request the identity number of the ETB the driver is calling from.'

'We ask this one even though the technology means we can see it straight away. We need verbal confirmation from the driver – everything is taped in case it's needed in court.'

'I see,' replied Andy.

She scrolled through the remaining questions. They established whether the vehicle was on the hard shoulder, if it was before or beyond the ETB, and what the nature of the problem was.

'The last thing to do is take their breakdown insurance details. Then you phone that info to the organisation they're with – we have direct-dial buttons on the phone – and get back to the driver with an estimated time of arrival for the rescue vehicle. Guidelines say no vehicle should be on the hard shoulder for more than half an hour, but with the traffic these days we allow an hour and a quarter. If there's no chance of a rescue vehicle before then, we phone the nearest police authority-approved garage to get the vehicle towed off. All clear so far?'

Andy nodded, battling his disappointment at being demoted to a phone operator. This wasn't why he'd sat the police exams.

'Next thing is to pass the incident details to the radio operator. Fill in the details here,' she pointed to the bottom part of her left-hand screen, 'then press "Send". That transfers the info to the radio operators in front of us. If it's necessary, the radio operator can then send a patrol car – or cars – to assist. And that's it.'

She smiled at him and he forced himself to grin back.

'Now we sit tight and wait for any calls to come in.' She picked up her nail file and began lightly brushing at the claw on her little finger. Andy sat listening to the quiet hiss of the headphones, and began to stare at the screens with their endless, silent film of moving cars. The morning dragged by and several times he caught his eyelids beginning to droop. It was nearly lunchtime before their headsets finally buzzed with an incoming call. Alice sat upright and pointed at the wall map. A tiny red dot was flashing on and off.

'Emergency Phone Operator,' she said in a neutral tone of voice.

'Hello? Hello!'

An engine roared past and the urgency in the caller's voice blasted away the cotton wool that had bloomed in Andy's head.

'Emergency Phone Operator, can you hear me?' Alice patiently repeated.

'Yes! Is that the AA?'

'No, I'm the Emergency Phone Operator. Can you tell me what number is written on the inside of the telephone box door?'

'Oh, right. Hang on. It's 133D!'

Andy looked at the wall and saw that the orange square by the red flashing bulb read 133D.

'Is your vehicle parked on the hard shoulder?' asked Alice.

'Yes! It's about 400 metres up the road.'

Alice worked her way through the list of questions while Andy sat in silence next to her. Once the caller had been dealt with Alice looked at him. 'See? Not so hard, is it? The screen has all the questions you need to ask. Now I'll pass it on to the radio operator.'

She typed a brief message into the bottom section of her screen and, as she pressed 'Send', said, 'It'll soon be time for lunch.'

In the afternoon Andy was moved to the front row of computers where he was seated next to a gaunt man with thinning hair. Once again he was given a pair of headsets with no mouthpiece. When the man spoke, it was fast. 'All right, Andy. My name's Greg. What brings you here?'

Andy coughed and began to reply quietly, 'Um, it's just a temporary thing. I've been off for a bit. They want to get me up to speed before, er, before I go back out on patrol. What about you?' He turned the conversation away.

'Me?' said Greg. 'I've worked here donkey's years. Love it. Technology's come a long way since I started here, I can tell you. Now we've got a lot more tools at our disposal.'

'So what do you do then?' asked Andy.

'Well, it depends on what's happened. If it's a Road Traffic Accident – RTA to you and me – we send a patrol car automatically. If it's congestion caused by, say, debris on the lanes, we'll assess the problem before sending a unit. Like a newspaper or something. No point in sending a unit then 'cos it'll be dispersed by passing traffic before the patrol car gets there. But, say, a dead deer in the slow lane? Send a unit, definitely – and put a closure on that lane.'

Andy sat back in his seat, relieved the man was off on a speech that needed no prompting.

'We do that by using the overhead signs. Simple, now it's com-puterised. Say the deer's on Delta stretch, by ETB 156D. Put that into the computer and select "Close lane". The nearest sign shows a circle with a cross in it, next one back shows a "Divert right" sign, next one back a "20 MPH", next two before that a "50 MPH". It's an offence for a vehicle to stay in a closed lane. Three points and seventy sheets if you do. So – in theory – when the unit gets to the incident, there shouldn't be any more cars driving over Bambi. Scrape him up and sling his remains on to the verge for crow food.'

He smiled triumphantly at Andy as a box lit up on his screen. Andy pointed to it and Greg turned his head back.

'Oh, a two-vehicle RTA on Lima. No serious injuries. One car sideways on in the slow lane, one pulled on to the hard shoulder. Right, listen and learn, mate. Lima stretch – that's between junctions one and nine over there.'

He pointed to the right-hand corner of the road map on the wall.

'Put that in,' he tapped the details in on his keyboard, 'and the computer tells us we've got two cars in the vicinity – driver 1214L1 and driver 1499L1. 1499L1 is in a Range Rover, so we'll send him to tow off the stationary vehicle.'

He pressed the 'Transmit' button in front of him and spoke into his mouthpiece. 'Base to driver 1499L1, we have a two-vehicle RTA just after junction 3, southbound. No serious injuries. One vehicle is stationary in the slow lane. Please proceed for an attend and tow.' He remained silent as the reply came in, then said, 'Roger 1499.'

Then he slipped his headset off. 'Right, you can send the other patrol car – just press the button and say, "Driver 1214L1, please also attend the RTA just after junction 3 southbound."'

Hurriedly Andy put the headset on, wondering why the number 1214 seemed familiar. He pressed the button and recited the sentence.

After a brief burst of static a voice said, 'Driver 1214L1, message received.' It was Walker's voice. Andy remembered 1214 was Walker's PIN number, he'd seen it on his shoulder tag. 'Am en route, five minutes away. Is that Constable Seer?'

Greg looked at him and began to nod. 'Yes,' Andy replied.

'Keep up the good work, lad.'

His ears burning, Andy whipped the headset off and handed it back to Greg. The thought of Walker out there on patrol as usual made him seethe with anger. The rest of the afternoon was spent brooding over Walker's comment until, eventually, he looked at the digital clock on the wall.

He removed his headset and held up his hand like a schoolboy. 'Excuse me, Mary – is it OK if I go? I've got that appointment in half an hour.'

'You get away, love. See you tomorrow.'

Andy quickly said goodbye to Greg, waved at Alice and then hurried from the room. The drive back into the city centre was against the flow of rush-hour traffic and he soon pulled up outside a stately terrace of houses. Most of the parking spaces were occupied by large expensive saloons or estates. Nothing too frivolous or sporty. Checking the numbers on the doors as he walked along, he noticed many bronze or brass plaques mounted on the walls by the buzzers. If they weren't doctors, they were solicitors. Eventually he reached number 62 and there, engraved on the obligatory metal plate amongst the names of the building's other occupants, were the words 'Dr K. Vashnay, AFBPsS'.

He pressed the buzzer and the door clicked, opening into a hallway painted in muted shades of blue with several doors leading off it. One of them opened and a tall, middle-aged man beckoned him in.

'Constable Seer, good to see you.'

They shook hands as he entered the room, Andy aware his hand was damp compared to the doctor's cool palm. He couldn't believe he was actually here, being assessed like a mental patient. Books lined one wall and he nervously looked around for a psychiatrist's couch.

'I'm afraid you don't get to lie on a chaise-longue,' said the doctor, smiling and pointing towards two chairs. They both sat down and the doctor crossed his legs. 'I gather you've been experiencing some trouble sleeping,' he said quietly, gazing at what looked like a leather-bound restaurant menu.

So, Andy thought, I'm his last dish of the day. He kept his hands still, wary of how any body movements might be interpreted, and cautiously replied, 'Yes, some. I think it's just getting used to the shifts I'm working now.'

'Yet you didn't experience the problem when working shifts in the supermarket, prior to joining the police?'

That was a warning shot for trying to fob the doctor off. Andy's face reddened. There was more in his notes than he'd realised.

'Your GP mentions that it's a problem you tend to experience when you feel under stress.' He peered at Andy over his glasses.

'Yes, I suppose that's true. I didn't sleep well when I did exams at school. And the same happened when I sat the police ones.'

'Mmmm – nothing too unusual there,' replied the doctor. 'And your present problems – do you think they're linked to the pressures of being in a new job or could there be an additional factor?'

Andy considered letting the counsellor know about his run-in with Ray Walker. But what if the doctor then included it in his notes? Inspector Marsh had already stated that he wanted to hear no more about the matter. 'I think it's the new job. I want to learn as much as I can, become the best officer I can. I suppose it makes me analyse things too much.'

'This analysing leads to your mind racing when you try to sleep?'

'Some nights.'

'And the incident in the patrol car. You'd dropped off and dreamt you'd seen some sort of camouflaged figure in front of the car?'

Andy felt a rush of resentment. 'Something like that,' he replied.

The doctor glanced at Andy's hands, and looking down he realised his thumb and forefinger were plucking at his other hand. Quickly he tucked both of them under his legs.

'Was the car parked in your real position or were you elsewhere during this dream?'

'We were parked on the concealed ramp on the hard shoulder, exactly where we were in real life.' Andy realised that by talking about Walker's lies as the truth he gave them credibility in his own mind. He added, 'It was all real as far as I'm concerned.'

The end of the doctor's pen swayed as he made rapid notes. 'Don't worry, it's common to experience mild hallucinations – visual or auditory – when suffering from nervous exhaustion. Let's go back to when you first saw your GP about the problem. She recommended that you . . .' He let the sentence hang so Andy could complete it.

'Try deep-breathing exercises, take those herbal relaxation tablets and do exercise. She suggested yoga, but I just go running instead.'

'Yoga can teach us to relax, that's for sure. Anything else?'

'To avoid all caffeine. You know, just buy decaff coffee and tea. And avoid those pep-you-up drinks too.'

'And these measures had no effect?'

'Not really.'

'OK, Andrew. Describe to me in more detail how you feel when you experience these sleepless nights.'

'Well, I generally know when I'll have one. I can be in bed, but my mind just won't slow down. It's like I'm seeing again on fast forward everything that's happened during the day. Things turn over and over in my head – stuff people have said, details about the day's incidents – and the more I try to sleep, the more impossible sleep becomes.'

'And this creates anxiety?'

'Yes. No. More frustration really. You know – the covers start bothering me and I get itchy. It gets worse and worse. Usually I give up and play on the computer in my room.'

'For how long?'

'Hours some nights.'

'Well, Andrew, by getting out of bed you're doing the right thing. But by playing on the computer you're doing the wrong thing. The trouble with lying in bed trying to force sleep to come is that you're creating a negative association in your head between sleeplessness and your bed. Your bed becomes part of the problem. What I want you to try is this. Next time you can't sleep, get up and sit on a chair facing the wall. Don't turn the light on, just sit still, breathe slowly and do nothing. The fact that you'll become uncomfortable, perhaps cold, is all right. What we want your mind to do is associate the chair with no sleep. Once you feel tired, return to your bed. As you warm up and relax your mind should start to form an association between bed, comfort . . . and healthy sleep. If your mind starts speeding up again, return to the chair.'

Andy tried not to look dubious. 'How long should I try this for each night?'

'As long as you previously spent playing computer games before sleep came. But I don't expect it to take that long.' He jotted down some more notes on the paper hidden behind the leather folder. 'OK, I'll see you again at the same time in another fortnight.'

'When can I resume full duties?' Andy asked.

'Hopefully, fairly soon. But we need to resolve this problem first and get your mind to accept the normal cues for sleep.'

'So how long could that take?'

'That's for you to tell me at your next appointment,' replied the counsellor, getting up.

They shook hands once again and Andy was shown back outside on to the street. Once on the pavement he felt like a leper, someone marred, marked out as faulty. He looked at his watch – there was still an hour or two more to lose before he could return home as if from a patrol shift. Feeling dejected, he walked slowly into the city centre. After a while he reached a small square and began following the signs for the library. The streets were now almost deserted, screens being drawn down over shop windows. He got to a fork in the path and had just decided on the footbridge when whispers from the mouth of the underpass drew him towards it. He stepped round the corner, almost into a couple of young lads spray-painting the tunnel wall. Automatically he shouted 'Oi!' and they dropped the can and sprinted off down the tunnel. The can rolled to his feet. Picking it up, he walked back up the curving path and out on to the footbridge. Halfway over he stopped. Leaning on the rails, he watched the traffic disappearing beneath his feet in a never-ending stream. Shutting his eyes and re-opening them a couple of seconds later made no difference; the flow continued. He imagined the city was a heart, sucking the mass of vehicles into its centre at the start of each day before pumping them back out at its end. The cars flooded along like blood cells in a vein, dispersing into the capillaries of roads and spreading through the surrounding area before being drawn back into the city again the next morning. And somewhere, carried along in this cycle, was the bad blood cell – the one carrying the killer. He frowned at the infinite flow of cars. None of them could even guess at what he knew. Yet here he was, unfairly barred from the job he'd yearned for, while everyone else carried on as normal. Ignorant of how he'd been cheated.

Filled with rage and frustration, he knelt down and pushed a hand between the railings. He began to spray in clumsy upside-down strokes, shuffling backwards on his knees every three or four letters so that, thirty foot later, the message was clearly visible to all three lanes.

He stood up and looked down at the traffic once again. As the cars approached him he could see one or two faces tilted up, the drivers regarding the figure above them. Probably wondering if he was about to jump. Andy took a sharp intake of breath and shivered, realising that he couldn't go on like this, allowing his sense of injustice and self-pity to drag him down. That way only led to the shame of total failure. He pictured his grandpa, and couldn't even begin to consider having to admit everything to him. The seed of resolve began to grow, and he knew what he must do. He would win back his place with the motorway traffic police before his grandpa arrived. And the only way to do that was by finding the killer himself.

He stared at the can of spray paint in his hand, then reached between the bars and let it drop towards the central reservation directly below. The can revolved slowly in the air then vanished soundlessly into the long grass. Filled with determination, Andy turned around and strode back the way he had come.

Chapter 28
The Searcher

Though his wrist was still too sore to drive, the compulsion to forage was growing stronger all the time. For large parts of the day he lay in his bed, dozing fitfully. Hunger constantly nagged at him and he drank large amounts of water from the bathroom tap to subdue the worst pangs. When he grew too restless he would pace the dim interior of the house, eyeing his collection and examining his bruise. Eventually his mind turned to a fairly good patch of road that was within walking distance, in a quieter part of the city. As he half-jogged along the side streets, cutting through alleys, he kept checking over his shoulder. But if they were following, they somehow kept out of sight.

What he was aiming for wasn't actually the central reservation, rather a triangular slope formed by a turn-off from the motorway. Though he'd brought his torch it wasn't really a proper forage either – for a start he wasn't even wearing camouflage paint. All he really wanted to do was lie in the long grass and listen to the passing traffic. The sound soothed him and made the events of the past few days seem far away.

Once he was safely on his territory, he worked his way through a patch of straggling ragwort stalks into the shadow of the bridge. Using the taller plants as cover, he rested his head on an outstretched arm, chewing on handfuls of grass and watching the passing headlights glimmering through the mesh of leaves. He didn't know how long he'd been dozing before the staccato drumming of tyres running over the white lines woke him. The headlights were on the hard shoulder, moving diagonally towards the grass verge. The car was going very fast.

He sat up, trying to gauge if it was going to roar up the slope, right at him. The bumper reared as it left the tarmac and he glimpsed the outline of the driver's head jerk upright. He must have been asleep too. Now the car was bouncing wildly across the grass and he realised that, though he was safe, it was careering straight towards the base of the bridge down the slope from him. He could see the driver's hands, white like little mittens, as he fought desperately to gain control of the car and steer it back towards the tarmac. It chewed up the remaining distance in no time and slammed into the bare concrete with a sickening metallic crack. The engine abruptly stopped and the lights went out.

He sat there looking from the wreck to the empty road behind and then, without thinking, scrambled down the slope to the vehicle's side. The bonnet was completely stoved in, bent back and up like the crumpled snout of a pig. He pulled at the passenger door but the frame had buckled and the door was stuck fast. Circling round to the front, he brushed diamonds of broken glass from the bonnet and climbed up. Ripping the masking tape from the torch's end, he leaned in through the shattered windscreen.

The light picked out the freshly tossed contents of the car and he was immediately snatched back to another car crash: the one where he'd killed his family.

He'd been on the back seat playing as usual with his Explorer Action Man. The figure was more than his favourite toy – it was a companion, fearless and faithful, who went with him everywhere. Around the garden, into the untended bush at the bottom, through the uncharted marshy land by the drain overflow, into the lost ruins of the derelict shed. So when his bored older brother had snatched it out of his hand, and with forefinger and thumb dangled it through the gap in the window on his side, a sickening fear had filled him. Maybe it was because he'd lunged at his brother's arm, or maybe his brother had let go of it deliberately, but the figure dropped from his fingers. Twisting in his seat, he watched through the back windscreen as the toy bounced along the road behind before catching an edge and spinning off into the grass of the central reservation itself.

When his mum had told him that they couldn't stop on the motorway, that retrieving it was impossible, he'd flown into a blind rage, clawing at his brother's eyes. She couldn't pull him off and that was when his dad half turned in his seat and, with one scrabbling hand, tried to grab him by his hair. He never exactly knew what happened, but the next thing his mother was screaming and they were floating, the pitch of the engine going high as the tyres left the road. His next memory was of the firemen cutting him free, his brother's mangled body pinned in his broken arms. And so he'd been left alone, with just the house, the money and a burning fixation with the land he'd lost his best friend to.

A groan brought him round and he directed the torch at the sound. The driver had been thrown forward and whiplashed back, no sign of a seat belt. Strands of hair from his pony-tail hung over his face and a rapidly blossoming red bib covered the front of his shirt. Bending through the remains of the windscreen he shone the light into the man's face. It was as if the impact, in a split second, had sucked almost all of the life out of him. The skin across his forehead and cheek bones was stretched so tight it looked like little more than a thin film of white rubber pulled over a skull. Stubble that a few minutes before had been beneath the skin now seemed forced out by the contraction. The same process had squeezed out little pinpricks of sweat across his face. Blood pumped in a steady flow from his forehead.

The light revived the driver and his eyes swivelled in their sockets to stare, unfocused, at the beam. The man licked his lips and then something else caught his attention and he looked feverishly above the torch, into the darkness beyond. Perhaps at death itself. Looking back at the light, the driver quickly began to whisper, 'Please help, please help, pleasehelp, pleasehelppleasehel . . .'

The words came out in little gasps, flowing into one sound,

coalescing in his head before separating out again as 'Hell please, hell please, hell please.'

For the first time in many years he began to giggle. The man had mistaken him for the agent – and not the witness – of his death! Back up the motorway headlights appeared. He shone the torch round the interior and the shaking light picked out a mobile phone held fast in its plastic holder on the dashboard. He snatched it for his collection and fled back up the slope.

He walked for a long time along the outskirts of the city, following the cycle paths until he found himself at the library. Through the dark glass he could see the emergency exit signs softly glowing green and the brilliant light of the aquarium as it bubbled on, oblivious to the lack of observers. From somewhere amongst the old industrial buildings that led down to the river he could hear a steadily beating drum. He turned away and walked on to the footbridge that spanned the dual carriageway. Midway across he stopped and looked down at the lit lanes below. Suddenly the mobile phone began to warble a little tune in his pocket. Checking there was no one near, he pulled the device out and looked at it. The back-lit screen was displaying the words 'Lucy. Answer?' He studied the little machine. Eventually its ringing stopped and the words were replaced by 'Answerphone. Message.'

The fear created by the ones who spied on him was now mixed with indignation, even anger, at the way they had terrorised him. He resolved then that, despite their efforts, he would return to the stretch of central reservation he had now twice been prevented from searching. And if his wrist allowed it he would go back on the date that his body clock dictated: the next full moon. He drifted over to the other side of the bridge.

Chapter 29
The Killer

'Sal, where's my passport?'

'Why? Where the bloody hell do you think you're going?' she answered from the kitchen.

'This delivery's to Scotland – how else will I get over the border?'

'Very funny, you big prat.'

'Right – I'll see you tomorrow morning,' he said through his smile, slamming the door shut behind him.

Once on the street he headed towards the lock-up but at the second corner doubled back and set off into the city, towards the river. It was 10.25. Ten minutes later he was jogging up the front steps of the club. Posters all the way down the street had proclaimed the night's event: 'Amok at the Shebeen. 11–7. Tickets £10 in advance, £15 on the door. DJs = Mr O, DJ Rim and Snooks.'

He banged on the metal-plated door, and a couple of seconds later an emaciated-looking girl struggled to pull it open. 'All right, how's it going?' She smiled, looking into his eyes with a warmth that was both totally welcoming and completely non-sexual. Clubber types always confused him. 'All right, cheers,' he replied flatly.

'Nice one.' She jabbed a cigarette towards the double doors at the other end of the foyer. 'Come in – they're all through there.'

He stepped into a mixture of smells. Stale beer and cigarette smoke lay behind the sharper scent of cleaning fluid. The mixture of aromas lent the air a heaviness, making it actually feel warmer in his nostrils. The carpet was patterned with a random array of cigarette burns and chewing gum marks; paint crinkled and peeled where the wall and ceiling met. He walked past the ticket booth and pushed open the double doors. The interior of the club was fully lit and he saw about a dozen figures standing at the bar. As he picked his way between the battered chairs and tables he recognised a few faces from the gym. Once he got on to the dancefloor Gav saw him and raised an arm. He didn't dare wave back in case it looked like some sad dance move. And he never danced. They clasped hands across the bar.

'Drink?' Gav asked.

Dave glanced down the bar to check what the others were having. 'A Diet Coke's fine, thanks.'

'Mary – sort him out with a pint of Coke, yeah?' He walked off down the bar and Jeff came over.

'All right, mate?' Dave asked.

'Yeah, great,' Jeff replied. 'How's the shoulder – ready to start training again soon?'

Dave began rubbing it. 'I hope so – it's doing my head in not being able to.'

'Yeah, I bet. Funny, isn't it?' he said, looking round. 'These places look such shit heaps when the lights are on.'

The bar-girl, peroxide hair pulled back almost as tightly as her gold lamé dress, pushed the drink across to him. Glitter sparkled on her cheekbones and shoulders.

'Ta, love,' Dave said, deliberately glancing at her arse as she turned round to carry on stocking up the fridges with the other bar staff. They chatted about nothing for a bit until Gav returned.

'Right, lads, here are your jackets and ear-pieces,' Gav called over as he dumped down a pile of shiny black bomber jackets. They all got off their stools and surrounded the table. 'They're all the same size, so no scrapping.'

One of the other guys from the gym passed him and Jeff jackets.

On the left breast the word 'Shebeen' was machine-stitched in red thread.

'Now, these ear-pieces are all fucked except for four of them, which me, Jeff, Alan and Herman will be wearing.' Dave glanced around until he saw one of the headsets being passed to a stooping great giant who looked just like the lumbering creature out of *The Munsters*. 'The rest of you wear the other ones anyway, they let the punters know we're organised.'

Gav was just opening his mouth to speak again when an explosion of music made him flinch. The top of his lip lifted in a sneer and he glared up at the DJ box. Two figures were hunched over the decks, nodding behind a screen of smoke. Gav waved both arms at them and the music abruptly dropped. 'Sorry, mate,' one called down.

Gav turned back to his audience. 'Fucking freaks,' he said under his breath. 'Me and Ian will do the front door until the rush dies down at around one. Jason, Phil, Jeff and Dave – you lot can be on male searches. Mary and her space-head mate who hasn't even shown up yet get to do the chicks. Dave, you haven't done searches before here so don't spend ages – just a quick pat down and send them in. If they're carrying it'll only be up their arses anyway. The rest of you are all on in here – you know the score. Any trouble, steam in and bundle them straight out the nearest fire exit. Right, ten minutes until opening so let's go.'

The ones picked for the foyer followed Gav across the dance floor.

Back through the double doors the two others sat down on a couple of stools and began shadow-boxing each other. Something about the way they were perched with just their upper bodies swaying reminded Dave of two freshly sprung jack-in-a-boxes. He and Jeff leaned against the wall, and as the music began thumping in the main area, Gav unbolted the front entrance and swung one of the doors open.

Twenty minutes later the first people began climbing the steps and Gav kept them waiting outside to build up a queue. The ones at the front chatted excitedly, the girls with their arms wrapped round themselves to keep warm in the cool night air. After a bit Gav stepped back into the foyer and announced into his head-mike, 'Right, they're coming in.'

The other doorman stepped to the side and the first few clubbers were beckoned through the door. Once in the foyer they were directed over to the booth where cash and flyers changed hands. Turning from the window they were confronted with the row of black jackets and all stopped talking and stepped hesitantly towards the line of men. Only Mary broke the silence by waving enthusiastically from the corner. 'Come on, girls – you've got me.' She started cackling like Barbara Windsor and the punters relaxed and began moving forwards.

Dave patted down the shirt of his first search, quickly pressing against the leg pocket of the person's combat trousers with his palm and then waving him through. More people were coming in from the night and the foyer's heavy smell began to be replaced by the scent of perfume, after-shave and, closer to their faces, the fruitiness of alcohol.

After a couple of hours the press of people at the top of the steps lessened. Soon they began to arrive in smaller groups and Dave and Jeff had time to look up and chat between searches. 'Faye, d'you wanna sort us out with some drinks, yeah?' called Gav to the girl in the booth. She disappeared from view then came out from the side door with a load of cans. 'Help yourself, boys.'

A little while later Gav turned to Jeff. 'Right – you take over the door, we only need three on searches now. I'll head inside. Couple more hours and you can break for some food. There's sandwiches in the back room.' As he opened the double doors a dense wall of sweet-smelling fog enveloped him. It washed into the foyer and around their knees as Gav stepped into the cacophony beyond.

Despite being on his feet, Dave began to feel groggy with sleep. He looked at his watch. Just after two. He knew from experience that the sleepy patch had normally passed by four. He sucked in a gulp of cold drink and swished it round his mouth.

Three lads, faces flushed with booze, were coming through the door. They handed in their tickets and stepped up to be searched.

Dave's wore a light cotton top with a big pouched front pocket. He slid his hands over the youngster's arms and then patted the pouch. A few things were inside. Dave reached in and pulled them out. Cigarettes. Lighter. Small aerosol can. He turned it in his fingers and read: 'Mace – devastating defence from personal assault.'

'What's this?' he asked.

'Tear-gas spray,' the lad answered. 'I'm a student,' he added by way of an explanation.

'I don't care if you're Alfred fucking Einstein, you're not taking that inside,' answered Dave, pocketing it.

'Albert. It was Albert Einstein,' the student replied, all confident and well educated.

Dave's face darkened. 'Right, let's see in your jeans pockets.'

The student pulled out a thin wallet. Dave snatched it and flipped it open. Inside was £30, a student union card, library card, cashpoint card and AA card. Dave tapped the AA membership card. 'Drive, do you?'

'Well, yeah,' replied the student.

'Ever had a crash?'

Confused, he looked towards the other bouncers for a clue as to what was going on. They stared impassively back. He looked again at Dave. 'Yeah. Just the one.'

'Whereabouts, on a motorway?'

'On a dual carriageway.'

'Caused a great fucking delay, did you? People stuck for hours because of you?'

The student again looked around him to see if this was some kind of joke. His mates stood silently to the side. 'No, someone shunted me. But there was a slight delay,' he replied hesitantly.

'A slight delay?' Dave hissed, eyebrows raised, one fist clenched. 'A slight fucking delay?' From the corner of his eye he felt Jeff's inquisitive stare. Getting a grip on himself he shoved the wallet back at the student and nodded him towards the inner doors. 'Fuck off inside.'

'Could I collect the spray at the end then?' the student asked politely.

'You'll be collecting your fucking teeth off the carpet at the end. Now piss off,' said Dave, pushing him towards the inner doors. His mates grabbed his arms and quickly directed him through.

The incessant beat from inside was beginning to get on Dave's nerves. The searching had dropped off almost completely when Jeff turned from the front door, hand up to his ear-piece. 'OK, Gav,' he said. 'Right – Jason, Phil, you can take twenty minutes – there's food in the store room behind the ticket booth.'

The pair opened the door marked 'Private' and went inside. People were now beginning to leave the main area, in total contrast to the way they'd entered. Wide-eyed and dishevelled, they emerged into the brighter lights, unsteady on their feet. Hair and T-shirts plastered in sweat. Many were chewing gum like Premiership football managers. They drifted towards the doors, arms round each other's shoulders, earnestly thanking the staff as they left the club. Pausing at the top of the stairs, they lit cigarettes and then faded into the night.

After a while Jason and Phil came back out.

'Come on, Dave,' said Jeff and they headed into the store room. A little table was wedged in front of a pile of toilet rolls and cases of floor cleaner. Packets of sandwiches and sausage rolls lay heaped in the middle. They sat down and Dave examined the 'contents' table printed on the wrapper of a pastry-covered lump. 'Fuck knows what they put in those things – except loads of fat.' He discarded it for some sandwiches and yawned. 'Shit, I'm knackered.'

'Yeah – it doesn't help it being a quiet night,' Jeff replied. 'There were a couple of big nights last weekend, it's probably cleaned most of them out until next pay day. What was all that about with the student earlier on?'

Dave looked up. 'When?'

'You know, all that stuff about the AA.'

Dave smiled. 'Fuck knows. I was just trying to put the shits up him. It was all I could think of.'

Jeff shook his head. 'I'd have just twatted the cocky little runt.'

He unfolded a copy of yesterday's *Sun*, then frowned and pressed the tiny microphone in his ear. 'Fucking great, Herman's got a puker in the foyer. I'd better go in.'

'Do you want a hand?' asked Dave.

'No, you're all right. It's only some girl, we'll just bung her out the side door. Back in a minute.'

The door shut and Dave leaned back, arms folded across his chest. The repetitive beat was now muffled to a level he actually found quite pleasant. It rolled on in bursts, occasionally varying in pitch and speed. His head gradually lolled forward and then he was standing in the doorway to his own front room. His daughter lay stretched out on her play mat on the floor, legs and arms splayed like an upturned frog. He floated towards her, bending down and bringing his face to within inches of hers and blowing softly on her cheek. She crinkled her nose and her fingers flexed. He blew harder; it was time for her lunch. Kitchen sounds, microwave pinging. She turned her head and he could see her eyes moving behind the lids with their delicate veins. Slowly the lashes moved apart and the eyes of the other girl he so wanted to forget looked up at him.

He shot up towards the ceiling, in a sickening, weightless lurch, head thrashing from side to side.

'Dave! Dave! For fuck's sake!' His eyes snapped open, someone was roaring and Jeff was shaking his shoulders. 'Easy, easy,' he was saying. The roaring stopped and Dave realised he'd shut his mouth. 'Jesus, I thought you were having a fit,' Jeff said, leaning forward, staring uneasily into his face. 'Are you all right?'

Dave grabbed his mate's forearm with both hands and began to stutter. 'I . . . I . . . I'm . . . I've . . .' A hiss of breath escaped from his gritted teeth, as he teetered on the precipice of his confession.

Sensing something terrible, his friend pulled his arm from the desperate grasp and straightened up. 'Listen, mate – go home. Call it a day.'

The urge fled back into the colossal fortress he'd built his body into. Unable to take eye contact, he bent forward and put his head in his hands. No words would come and the seconds passed in silence. Eventually he breathed deeply and raised his head. 'Sorry, mate. I'm wasted at the moment. Bills. Money. Driving all the time. I'm sorry.'

'Don't worry about it. I'll square it with Gav and make sure you get your cash. Come on, call it a night. Just head straight for the door – I'll take care of everything.'

Dave mutely slipped off the jacket and headset. 'OK, thanks,' he meekly replied.

Jeff led him out to the main door. 'See you at the gym, mate,' he said cheerfully. Dave waved a hand and walked slowly down the steps, glad of the cold air. Street lights bathed the pavement orange, and as he walked up the road he watched his shadow stretching out and contracting back as he passed each lamp. He breathed deeply and waited for his pulse to slow.

At the top of the road the footpath began. He turned away from the sign for the library, and instead took the path leading to the footbridge. Keeping one hand on the railing, he carefully stepped out on to the walkway, reassured by his grip on the rough sandpaper surface. Just after the bridge's highest point he paused and looked down at the lanes below. A few cars sped along, their colours all turned to a similar dull shade by the motorway lighting. He placed both hands on the rail and braced his legs. The faint thud of the club music was carried to him on the light breeze. Filled with hate, he watched the vehicles as they approached, bowing his head to see them disappear beneath his feet.

And gradually, as he stood there staring down, it seemed as if the bridge, not the cars, was moving. Slowly at first but with a quickly increasing momentum, he started rolling forwards. Looking up he imagined he was astride a terrible machine, standing triumphantly at its helm, directing its unstoppable advance. Effortlessly he glided onwards, swallowing vehicle after vehicle into the cavernous space below. The wind rushed against his face, tears streamed from the corners of his eyes. Below, cars swerved out of the lane which led directly below the rigid silhouette. But whichever lane they switched to, they couldn't avoid driving under the ominous spray-painted message that read 'DRIVE YOURSELVES TO DEATH'.

Movement beside him brought him back to reality. A couple of clubbers were skirting nervously around him, pressed against the other side of the walkway. He realised he was gasping for breath, legs apart, arms straight out before him, railings gripped in a white-knuckled clench. He waited for the two of them to disappear. Then, deciding that it was time to hunt again, he marched on, over to the other side.

Chapter 30
The Hunter

He opened the front door and bounded up the stairs two at a time. Once inside his room he shut the door behind him and sat down on the bed. From the shopping bag on his lap he took out a thickly folded rectangle of paper and looked around at the walls. Then he knelt on his bed, tearing down several of the old car posters he had pinned there as a teenager. Scrunching them into balls, he dropped them into the bin by his computer. Next he unfolded the Ordnance Survey map and, emulating his Inspector, pinned it up in the space he'd just created.

With his finger he traced the M40 along its downward curve towards London. There were the services, so he'd gone too far. Moving back he found junction 14, and keeping one finger on the spot just beyond it, he lifted the rest of his hand away from the wall to examine the land bordering the motorway itself. They'd been on the westbound hard shoulder when the figure had appeared – somewhere within three miles of the junction. He pored over the land to the side of the motorway lanes; fields, an isolated farm building or two. And a track. It branched off a tiny B-road and ran parallel to the motorway for a few hundred yards before petering out in some empty fields. A mile or so on and several fields later the dotted line reappeared, meandering along to join another B-road that led into a tiny village called Eskwith.

Just under an hour later he was pulling up at the mouth of the track. He turned the car's lights off and sat back, staring into the blackness around him, soaking up the silence. Cautiously he opened the door, climbed out. As he gently clicked it shut, a shriek rang out from above; startled, he dropped the car keys. The disturbed owl moved off to hunt somewhere else, repeating its mournful call a couple of fields away.

Bending down to retrieve his keys he noticed a small sausage-like lump lying next to them. He picked both objects up, pocketed his keys and then turned the lump over in his hands. It felt as if it was fashioned from velvet, with all sorts of tiny rigid objects packed beneath the surface. He stepped out from the shadows of the trees and into the dull moonlight for a better look. The surface was a furry patchwork, and here one of the inner objects poked through, bleached white. He got his keys back out from his pocket and used the end of one to part its surface. Inside was a compact cluster of minute bones, including a little skull. Even though Andy now recognised it as an owl pellet, no doubt disgorged from a feeding perch in the trees behind him, it seemed to him more like a hex. Some sinister voodoo fetish, moulded by a malevolent hand, warding him off from this deserted place. Tossing the lump aside, he dismissed the paranoid notion from his mind and then stood a little awkwardly, hands in his pockets.

He wasn't sure exactly what he was looking for as he stared down the dark lane. It appeared empty as far as he could see. He trod carefully along the grass verge lit by the silvery moonlight, careful to avoid any loose stones. Off to his left, he could hear the hum of traffic on the motorway. After walking for about five minutes the track ended at a low hedge, on the other side of which lay more empty fields. Beyond them he knew the track eventually reappeared and led to the village of Eskwith.

With head lowered, he turned round and retraced his steps, stopping about a third of the way back. The gravel had been disturbed – and where the stones had been moved he could see the mark of a tyre tread pressed into the earth. He looked towards the motorway and climbed over the fence. Carefully he picked his way through the high grass, climbing between some tight strands of wire halfway across. At the other side of the field he looked down the slope to the motorway and saw the concealed ramp where he and Walker had parked just a few weeks ago. The cows were gone now, but their hoof marks were still visible in the turf all around him. He remembered slapping one of the animals as it had leaned over the fence and curled its tongue at his torch.

Turning around, he made his way back towards the track. As he reached the wire fence halfway across, he leaned forward and pushed up the top strand with an outstretched arm. Crouching down, he got his first foot through and placed his other hand into the grass to steady himself. Something like a tube of lipstick dug into his palm, so he plucked it from the greenery and slipped it into his coat pocket.

Back in his car he turned on the interior light then, with forefinger and thumb, carefully removed the tube and held it under the weak light.

Watson's camouflage cream. Dun green.

Struggling to control his excitement, he placed it upright on the dashboard, then took out some evidence bags and crumpled latex gloves from his coat. Sharply he blew into the gloves, causing the rubber fingers to spasm then collapse back. He slipped both on, then took out a Swiss Army knife and unfolded the smallest blade. Lightly gripping the tube by its base, he delicately prised up the lid and transferred it by the tip of the blade on to the passenger seat. Holding the tube closer to the light, he squinted at it and his eyes widened.

Quickly he put the tube back on the dashboard, pulled the tweezers from the penknife and turned on the torch. But now he discovered he couldn't hold the torch, tweezers and tube simultaneously. He tried balancing the torch on the dashboard but it kept rolling off, so instead he clamped it between his teeth. Then, bending his head close to the tube, he used the tweezers to extract a single hair from the waxy rime caught in the ridge of the tube's neck. The short brown hair hung stiffly before him: genetic evidence of the killer. Carefully Andy placed it in an evidence bag, did the same to the tube, and sealed them up. He pulled off the gloves and sat triumphantly back in his seat – now he'd discovered one of the killer's attack spots, he just had to work out when he was going to use it next. Desperately hoping it was before his grand-father's visit, he pushed the evidence bags back into his coat, where they nestled amongst the forgotten club flyers still in his pocket.

Chapter 31
The Searcher

The departures board was almost black. As he looked at it another column fluttered and spun, the little vinyl flaps only stopping once all the white writing had disappeared. Unable to resist the compulsion to forage any longer, he had walked to the rail terminal, timing his visit for the very end of the night. A few people hurried past on to platforms, and once he found the station name he was looking for, he also left the main hall to the man silently sweeping the floor.

His carriage clunked and rocked as it left the station, empty except for himself. He stared out of the window, sometimes at occasional lights shining beyond the glass, sometimes at his own ghost-like reflection as it swept across the black landscape. He kept count of the stations they stopped at, so when the momentum slowed for the sixth time, he stood up and was waiting at the doors well before the train actually came to a halt. The light behind the Open button glowed. He pressed it and stepped down on to the deserted platform. Behind him the doors slid shut and the train rattled on its way. He regarded the locked ticket office and wondered how to get out, then saw the side-gate pinned open with a loop of chain.

He went through and walked across the middle of the car park, on to the quiet street. To his left the village high street began; a little way down, tell-tale cracks of light gleamed through the curtains of a pub. He turned in the opposite direction and strode through the village outskirts and into country lanes. After half an hour he heard the familiar low drone and so climbed over the next gate in the high hedge that bordered the road. On the other side he slipped the small rucksack off his back and pulled on his army overalls, testing the pain in his wrist as he did so and wondering how soon he would be able to drive again.

Next he reached for the breast pocket, noticing the zip was slightly open. He inserted a finger into the gap and pushed the two rows of teeth apart, reaching inside for his tubes of cam-cream. One was missing. Frowning, he quickly covered his hands and face with broad strokes of the remaining two colours and then carried on. The field had been saturated by heavy rain, and after just a few steps his shoes and lower legs were soaked through. The motorway was a couple of hundred yards ahead, raised above the surrounding marshy land by an embankment. The field itself was more a series of shallow bumpy ridges that gave the land a rippled appearance when viewed from the road. Dotted about were clumps of tubular reeds, some of which bore spiked seed pods near the top. He plucked one of the stalks and split it open with his nail. Packed inside the fibrous green casing was a white spongy material. By squeezing it he forced a droplet of moisture out into the valley of his forefinger and thumb. He looked at the shining surface and saw a tiny moonlit sky captured in its quivering curve. Then he licked the miniature universe away, noting that it tasted quite sweet. As he went on a batch of frogs called excitedly to each other in the dark, their chorus of croaks sounding like a series of high-pitched burps. The squelch of his footsteps silenced them, and as he passed he imagined the bulbous eyes following him. A few steps further on and they started up again.

At the base of the slope leading up to the motorway he paused, this time his interest taken by a dark opening in the ground just off to his side. He went over to it and ran his hand around the concrete lip, remembering reading about such a thing in the library. It was a tunnel specially built for animals – badgers, foxes, hedgehogs and the like – to save them from the dangers of the motorway lanes above.

He looked into its narrow entrance and could just see a greyish glimmer at the other end. Tentatively he poked his head in, immediately aware that the air was slightly colder inside. His torch-light revealed small piles at the entrance and he recognised the acrid scent of fox droppings. The roof was too low to for him to enter on all fours so he wriggled in on his stomach, smearing excrement down his front. Once in, he propelled himself along in the same way as he did on the central reservation, shining his torch around, breathing in the dank air and examining the lichen and moss that hugged the rough concrete surface. He reached a slight dip in the middle that was filled by a shallow, stagnant puddle. Easing himself through it, he further coated himself in slime. Every so often a low rumbling would approach, reaching a crescendo over his head as the vehicle passed by just a few feet above.

At the other end were more piles of droppings and beyond similar marshy fields. Rain had begun to drop silently from the sky again so he emerged, quickly turned round and re-entered the hole. Soaked in slime and animal shit, he burrowed forward, the exertion forcing an occasional grunt from his lips. Well into the tunnel he stopped and rolled on to his back to enjoy the feeling of concealed proximity to the vehicles passing above. Here, below ground and hidden from the world outside, he felt for the first time in many weeks completely safe.

Chapter 32
The Killer

He stopped between the outer and inner doors of the wine bar and rummaged in his pocket for some small change. Once he'd dialled the number he pulled open one of the inner doors to increase the sound of loud music and voices from inside. It rang four times before his wife answered.

'Hi, Sal, can you hear me all right?'

'Yeah, just about. How's it going?'

'Good – they've given us jackets and headsets. All very professional. I tell you what – things are different nowadays. They're only just starting to queue up now and it's nearly midnight.'

'I know, I was just going to bed.'

'Right. Well, anyway, I'm going to be helping with the clear-up at the end too. So I won't be back until morning, OK?'

'Yeah, 'course.'

'Good. How's things?'

'Fine, I'm just watching the end of some film . . .'

'That's the pips,' he interrupted. 'See you tomorrow.'

'Night, hon.'

He hung up and walked back through the outer doors. That was the whole night freed up for a bit of sport. The van's engine roared into life and he drove back on to the motorway, wipers moving steadily back and forth.

The carton gurgled desperately for air as he sucked the last droplets out of it. Pushing the straw from between his lips, he flicked the small box out of the window towards the barriered strip of grass shooting along on his right.

He'd left the motorway system and had followed the A12 nearly as far as Ipswich before he saw the hazard lights winking at him through the misty sheets of drizzle. He dropped his speed but kept in the slow lane, examining the car in his rear-view mirror once he'd passed it. One person, in the passenger seat. He took the next exit, went round the roundabout and rejoined the road going in the opposite direction. At the next exit he came off again and then parked in a big layby, pulled on the boiler suit and removed his hunting kit from the back of the van. A quick U-turn and within five minutes he was pulling up behind the Citroën, yellow light flashing on the roof above.

He picked up his clipboard and climbed out into the damp night. He could see the occupant of the car looking round at his approach, but the car door didn't open. He walked up to the window, bent forward and mouthed the word 'hello'.

A nervous-looking elderly man stared back at him through the droplet-covered glass. He held up both hands, and with each fore-finger and thumb made a box shape in the air whilst saying the words, 'ID, please,' his voice muffled by the glass barrier between them.

Dave nodded, and using the palm of his hand smeared the rain across the glass to further obscure the driver's view. Then he held up his clipboard with an old delivery order on it. The vapour in the air had settled on the thin paper, making it wrinkle and curl. The man squinted at it, unable to make out any writing.

Wiping a raindrop from the end of his nose, Dave raised his voice and said, 'If you lower the window a little, sir, I could pass the breakdown order through to you.'

The man stopped squinting at the sheet and nodded. The window lowered by about six inches and he said, smiling awk-wardly, 'I'm sorry, you must understand my being careful.'

'Not at all sir, we've been instructed to be exactly the same. Here you go.' He held the clipboard up to the gap, and at the last second whipped out the can of Mace hidden behind it and sprayed directly into the man's eyes. He gasped at the searing pain and Dave aimed more liquid into his mouth. The man doubled forward, retching.

Quickly Dave reached through the window, popped the lock and opened the door. The driver fell out on to all fours, helpless, blind and convulsing. The tool-box clicked open and the monkey wrench came out.

Dave stood sideways on, flexed his knees and swung the wrench across his body like a golfer driving up the range. The tool reached its nadir and then rose upwards, connecting with the man's face, snapping his head backwards. A gout of puke and snot looped out, landing across Dave's foot. The man's head flopped forwards again – a wide open fissure stretching from his hairline to the bridge of his nose – and a thick fan of blood coated Dave from his knees down. The man's elbows buckled outwards and he collapsed face first on to the tarmac like someone praying to Mecca.

'You dirty bastard,' said Dave, totally outraged, looking down at his lower legs. 'You dirty fucking bastard!' Much louder. He turned on the figure, and keeping his double-handed grip on the heavy tool began furiously raining blows down on to the man's head.

Back in his lock-up he took off his trainers, shrugged his shoulders out of the boiler suit and kicked his feet free of the legs. The old man's temple had parted like a ripe melon and blood had covered his arms and chest, ruining the overalls. He screwed them up into a ball and threw it into the corner, knowing he already had a new pair waiting for him in his van. Then he stepped over to the tiny sink and bent forward to inspect his face in the mirror. As he'd suspected it was peppered with blood spots, so he turned on the single tap and held the old rag under the water. After scrubbing his head and face clean he turned his attention to his hands, rubbing between the fingers and working a brush at his nails until the residue of blood beneath them had been reduced to thin black lines.

Next were his trainers. They looked like he'd been splashing around in a muddy field. He picked one up and placed it in the sink. Briskly he began rasping the stiff bristles across the clogged surface, removing clumps of hair, clots of blood, shards of skull, shreds of brain. A tooth clattered on to the porcelain and rolled down the plug hole. It took a good five minutes of hard scrubbing to remove the mess. He placed the trainer to one side and with a sigh put the other one into the sink and started again.

After one final check in the mirror he lifted up the door, pulled the light off and locked up. Halfway home he stopped at a cashpoint, withdrew £70 and then continued on his way. When arriving back first thing in the morning, he always let himself quietly into the flat. Silence. He checked his watch, removing a speck of blood from its face. 6.38 a.m. A few minutes before Sal got up. When he stepped into the kitchen he was surprised to see her sitting in the gloom at the kitchen table.

He let out a long sigh, and rubbed the back of his neck. 'Jesus, what a night. I've had enough dance music crap to last me months. Mmm da, mmm da, mmm da, all fucking night.' He turned on the light. 'How are you anyway, doll?' As he stepped towards the kettle he tried to stroke her neck, but she shied away from his hand.

'Dave, if you're having an affair, I want you to tell me now.'

He looked at her blankly. Then she held up Gav's Peacemakers business card. 'According to this, the all-nighter at the Shebeen was on the fourteenth. So what are you playing at?'

Dave took the card from her hand, looked at Gav's writing on the back and smiled.

'You should get out more. Sitting around getting paranoid. This month's all-nighter was last night. The date written here is for next month's. When,' he pulled the wad of ten-pound notes from his pocket, 'another seventy quid is coming our way.'

He dropped the money on the table, then sat next to her and said more softly, 'Babe, I can't believe you'd think I was fooling around.'

Her rigid posture gave way and she leaned on his arm. 'God, I feel stupid. I've been sat here half the night feeling sick. I'm really sorry, Dave, I . . .'

He told her to hush, stroking the back of her lowered head. After a few moments she looked up. 'Your trainers are soaking.'

'I know, some pisshead puked all over them last night. I've

washed most of it off, but they still smell a bit.'

'Give 'em here then – I'll put them on a rinse for you. God, I'm sorry, Dave.'

'Don't be,' he said, making sure he looked slightly hurt. He undid the laces and handed the trainers to her. She threw them in the washing machine, poured in a dash of powder and turned the dial. Dave waited behind her until the drum started to revolve.

'Nice one, I'll grab a shower.'

He walked out of the kitchen and the bathroom door clicked shut. Seconds later the flames in the boiler flared as the hot water was turned on. Sally looked awkwardly around her, then turned the radio on.

'. . . *though the police haven't confirmed it yet, all early indications suggest that last night's victim was also killed by the Motorway Murderer. Once again the body was discovered by the driver of a motorway rescue vehicle. The dead man was lying on the near side of the car, which had broken down on the A12, about nine miles outside Ipswich. The rescue vehicle driver is currently in Ipswich Hospital, where he's being treated for shock.'*

With fingers nervously turning the pendant at her throat, Sally stared at the radio, at the money on the table, then at the radio again.

Chapter 33
The Hunter

He glanced cautiously across the canteen and caught Walker's eye for a split second. The faintest smirk tweaked the older man's fat lips before he turned back to the colleagues alongside him. Miserably Andy glanced at the middle-aged women he was sharing a table with. Mary looked at him and tried to involve him in the conversation, failing to hide the sympathy in her voice.

'Did you see *Brookside* last night, Andy? The way that new family are carrying on?'

He smiled regretfully and shook his head. 'No, I don't follow the soaps.' Heads turned away from him and he realised he'd just eliminated himself from their main topic of conversation. He tried to rectify the situation by saying, 'Are they turning out to be troublemakers then?'

But the interest in his voice didn't ring true and the curt agreement that followed was hardly directed at him. He suddenly knew that his sitting with these women was as much of a burden to them as it was to him. Having to spend their lunch hour with some young male, dumped with them only because he was too stressed to be out on the roads, hardly helped with their lunchtime conversations – at least not while he was actually sitting next to them.

A burst of raucous laughter rang out from the other side of the canteen and before he could help himself Andy looked across at

Walker. He sat there, with head tipped back and mouth open, his throat wobbling as he released his guffaws like an enormous belch. Andy realised he was looking down his nose directly at him. The joke, he concluded, was surely on him. Next thing he was on his feet, and with eyes fixed on the older man he calmly approached Walker's table.

'Having a good laugh?' asked Andy, eyebrows raised and an inquisitive smile on his face. Everyone at the table glanced towards him and some of the men, realising who had asked the question, looked down in embarrassment. From the far end someone whispered, 'Shit.'

Wiping a tear from the corner of his eye, Walker replied with a measured joviality, 'Yeah, we are. Thanks for asking.'

The smile vanished from Andy's face and when he spoke his voice was hard. 'About me, was it? Your little joke. So what sort of bullshit are you spreading about now, you scheming turd?'

The table looked at him in astonishment and the conversation around the rest of the canteen faded to silence. Walker struggled to push his chair back from under the table. He heaved himself to his feet and held his arms out. 'Look, Andy, go and sit down. You know you're meant to be keeping your distance – not having another go at me.'

'And why should I do that when you sit there grinning across at me like a fat idiot?'

'Andy, this isn't doing you any favours.' Walker stepped back closer to the wall and angled his body so the rest of the canteen could only see his profile. 'You need to calm down, mate.' Then he added, 'No one is trying to get at you,' and slowly winked at Andy with the eye his audience couldn't see.

The action provoked the desired response. Andy's fury boiled over. 'You, you . . .' But he couldn't get his brain in gear, and ended up just jabbing Walker in the chest.

The older officer had got his result: physical contact had been made. Andy was instantly forgotten as he now addressed his watching colleagues directly. 'I'll need you all to verify that – abusive behaviour and aggressive physical contact.'

One or two hesitantly nodded, but the majority did not respond. Instead they were looking expectantly at Andy, waiting for his next comment. He realised Walker had made a mistake trying to involve them; their sympathy wasn't completely with the older officer. Regaining some composure, he said, 'Don't try dragging them in with that shit. This is between us. You reckon you've stitched me up – but you're wrong.'

Walker dragged his eyes away from his colleagues and looked at Andy. 'What?'

'I said, you're wrong. I've been back to the place where I saw him. And I've found some evidence. Something that would stand up in court.'

Walker felt his face flush. he couldn't afford to have this conversation. Not in front of so many people. 'If you won't leave me alone, fine. But I'm not staying here listening to this crap.' He began trying to retreat towards the doors by squeezing along the gap between the chairs and the wall – but the space was too narrow for his bulk.

'Yeah, yeah. Avoid the discussion,' Andy said to his back. 'But the truth will out.'

'Move in a bit, Stuart, for fuck's sake!' Walker snapped, pushing at the back of the officer in the first chair. The seated man shuffled forward a bit and Walker was able to make some progress.

'You hear me, Walker? The truth will out,' Andy repeated slowly.

Walker struggled past the last chair, red-faced and clearly flustered. Waving the comments away, he stormed from the room.

Andy looked around the silent canteen, full of people uneasily toying with their cutlery. Addressing the room in general he said, 'Sorry you all had to sit through that,' then headed towards the swing doors himself.

Chapter 34
The Searcher

The last of the flies had finally died. Brittle husks lay scattered across every windowsill in the house. He'd walked from room to room poking at the piles with an outstretched finger; a couple of days ago the action would create flickering leg movements in a few, even the odd slow buzz of wings. But now the house had settled back to its former hush. Even the mobile phone was silent.

The way it had persisted with its warbling ring for the first few days after he'd acquired it had unsettled him. At first when it rang the screen would always read 'Lucy. Answer?' But later it had changed to 'Anonymous. Answer?' Other times it would just beep three times and, watching it through the side of the Perspex box, he noticed a little envelope emblem on the screen. He'd try to imagine who might have sent it. Then, eventually, 'Battery Low' appeared and one morning when he went to look at it, he found the screen was dead.

Now he sat on his kitchen chair, flexing his wrist and staring impassively at the calendar on the wall. The red felt-tip circle round the date of the next full moon was the only thing marked on the sheet. The night edged ever closer.

Chapter 35
The Killer

'What's the matter?' he said groggily, turning his head on the pillow.

She stopped prodding him and said, 'Hon, I can't sleep with it. It makes my hair stand on end.'

'What are you on about?'

'You grinding your teeth. The noise is horrible – like two pebbles being rubbed together.'

'Was I?' he asked, coming fully awake. The usual stabbing sensations were shooting through his jaw muscles, and when he tried to open his mouth the pain instantly intensified. A headache hovered eagerly behind.

'When can you start going to the gym again? I'm sure it's why you've started grinding your teeth – you've got too much energy bottled up.'

She was right. He hadn't been to the gym for well over a fortnight; it was the longest he'd gone without a proper workout for years. The resulting restlessness was even making sleep hard. 'I'll go again as soon as I can,' he answered quietly.

His wife looked at the alarm clock and sat up. 'It's 6.15, Jasmine will be awake soon. And that's another thing – you've gone all funny with her too.'

'How do you mean?' he asked sharply.

'Well, you're too uptight ever to play with her. I don't think you've even touched her in days. Maybe you should go and see the doctor about grinding your teeth. It can't be doing them any good. And all your pacing round the flat certainly isn't doing me any good.'

'Yeah, don't worry. I'll sort out something,' he replied, eyes fixed on the bedroom ceiling.

Chapter 36
The Hunter

Cars parked in the fast lane. Vehicles reversing back up the hard shoulder. Fluttering documents being chased on to the central reservation. Grainy footage of people steering with their knees while eating sandwiches. A van swerving across two lanes, sending a lorry crashing off the motorway.

Shaking his head, he pressed the Stop button and his *Police! Action! Live!* video whirred to a stop. He switched the TV off and quietly climbed the stairs. In his room he quickly stripped down to his boxer shorts and got into bed. He lay on his back, allowing himself to sink into the mattress, concentrating on getting all his muscles to relax. Slightly pursing his lips, he pulled air deep into his lungs and slowly let it out. He repeated the breathing exercise four more times, then lay still. But his mind raced on, analysing, examining, replaying. Snippets of conversations, images of the hard shoulder, sentences from newspaper reports. He picked over everything, desperately searching for any clue as to when the killer might strike next. His feet felt hot and irritably he kicked at the duvet. Then the backs of his arms began to itch.

Not allowing the process to begin, he threw the duvet off him, climbed out of bed and sat in his chair. After turning the lamp on he started up his computer, staring resignedly at the screen. 'Hello,

Andy. The harvest festival of Lugnasdh is exactly four weeks away. What can I do for you today?'

As usual, he dismissed the wizard and started up Joy Rider. He selected the motorway scenario and chased a Sierra Cosworth for miles around a spaghetti junction while a police helicopter kept the car illuminated in a brilliant white spot. When his fingers and neck began to ache he froze the game, stretched out his arms and began to crack his knuckles. It was hopeless trying to deduce when the killer would attack again.

He decided to try the counsellor's advice and sit in the dark, so shut down the game and turned the computer off. As he reached for the lamp he caught sight of the evidence bags lying on top of the club flyers by the side of his monitor. On impulse he slid the bags aside and picked up the pile of cards. Absently he began flicking through them again.

'Revelation at the Shebeen. £6 before 10 p.m. with this flyer.'

'Excess at Cartagena. £5 & free drink before midnite with this flyer.'

'Eden at the Promise. Drinks promos all night. £2 off entry with this flyer.'

The card felt thicker than the others and he realised it was in fact two, stuck together. Peeling them apart he looked at the second.

'Full Moon Wobbler at Trifle. £5 Fri & Sat plus a free drink both nights with this flyer.'

Andy looked at the computer screen, turning the card over and over in his hand. Full moon. There was something about that date to do with his computer. A mental image of the little wizard slowly detached itself and floated free from the morass of other memories. The cape swirled and the figure vanished. He remembered that something major had coincided with the last two times he'd appeared with his message about the full moon. He searched his mind. The last time was when he'd got in after being betrayed by Walker, the night he'd seen the camouflaged figure on the hard shoulder. He reversed back through the weeks preceding that night and his mind finally stopped at the memory of sitting in front of his computer after the killing at junction 14. The wizard had appeared with his full moon message that morning too. He thought: the dates the killer strikes on the M40 coincide with the full moon.

He jumped to his feet and scrabbled for his diary on the bookshelf. Swiftly turning pages, he shot through the last weeks of his attachment, shifts filling the sheets as blue felt-tip lines. As he went further on the markings stopped and page after page of empty white space followed. He reached the present date and scanned over the next few days before realising his diary didn't indicate which nights the full moon fell on. Throwing it back on the shelf, he rushed from his room and raced down the stairs. In the kitchen he yanked the calendar off the cork board and sat at the table. His forefinger roved across the grid of days on the sheet to the present date and paused. Holding his breath, he moved his finger down and there, in just two nights' time, were the words he was hoping for: full moon. Then, as he read his mum's addition to the box, his rush of excitement instantly turned to horror. 'Grandpa driving up from Dover.'

He'd heard the canteen reports about the ferocity of the latest killing. The stuff you don't read about in the papers. Chips taken out of the tarmac where the madman had carried on battering the skull long after it was reduced to little more than a lumpy paste. Awful images of his grandpa flashed through his mind. Waiting patiently for the rescue vehicle as the camouflaged monster silently descended from the bank above. The door being yanked open and his frail form dragged from the car. The bludgeoning onslaught, the splintering bones; the phone rang for almost three minutes before it was answered.

'The Beeches. Can I help you?'

'Yes,' Andy answered, 'I urgently need to speak with Alfred Seer, Flat 2.'

'It's gone midnight. He's in bed. We're all in bed.'

'I'm sorry. Please, tell him it's his grandson, Andy. It's very urgent.'

'I'll try.'

While he waited the ceiling creaked as someone stirred above him.

'Andy, is that you?' His grandfather's croaky voice coming down the phone line.

'Yes, Grandpa. It's me. Listen – you mustn't drive up this Wednesday night.'

'Andrew, slow down. What's the matter?'

'Nothing. Everything's fine.' He shut his eyes and pressed his forehead against the wall. 'It's just Wednesday night's not, not . . . a good night.'

'Why? Is your mother not well?'

'No. No, she's fine as well. We're all fine. But that night – it's not suitable.'

'Nonsense, Andrew. I've arranged everything. Bob's looking after Prince while I'm away. Your mum's expecting me, and I've got lots to ask you. Have you just come off shift, by the way? It's very late, you know.'

He pressed the receiver against his temple, knowing he'd never dissuade the old man from setting off. A pair of feet had now stopped at the top of the stairs.

'Look, Grandpa, you shouldn't use the motorways. Especially the M40. Use minor roads instead.'

'Andrew, you're not making sense. Are you all right? Is your mother there?'

'No, she isn't. Please – you must check your car before you set off. Oil, water, tyres.' He repeated advice back at the man who had originally given it to him. 'It's . . . it's dangerous to be travelling at night.'

'Oh, that. Don't worry, Andrew. We'll talk tomorrow. Now I must go, I'm disturbing people here. I'll see you soon.'

He hung up and Andy returned the phone to its cradle.

'Andrew, what was all that about?' He could see his mum's bare feet between the banisters as he walked into the sitting room.

'Nothing, don't worry. Go back to bed,' he replied, shutting the door behind him. Standing at the window he stared up in anguish at the night sky and decided that the best way to protect his grandfather – and redeem himself – was to stake out the killer's attack point on the M40.

Chapter 37
The Searcher

Labels were pulled out from a thick roll and waxy paper carefully snipped with surgical scissors. Dust-coated boxes covered the kitchen table before him, faded labels half hanging off the sides. He removed one of the curled scraps and placed it on the table. The faint writing read 'Adidas trainer, size 4. Made in the Philippines.'

He lined up a new label and carefully transcribed the message on to it in his tiny and precise hand. Then he folded up the old one and dropped it into the bin by his side. He picked up the box, wiped the grime and dust from its sides with a damp J-cloth, dried it with a tea towel, and carefully stuck the new label on the lid. He repeated the process, patiently writing out new labels, again and again:

'Pebble Prominent Moth. *Eligmodonta ziczac.*'

'Marlboro Lights, twenty. Philip Morris Products Inc.'

'Gout weed, seed head. *Aegopodium podagraria.*'

'Common Bluebell. *Hyacinthoides non-scriptus.*'

'Bic, blue. Medium.'

'Wrigley, Orbit. Sugarfree gum.'

He paused in his writing to look at his hand, flexed his fingers and rotated his wrist. He realised the pain was almost gone and it felt good enough to drive again.

Chapter 38
The Killer

He sat waiting for her. Balanced on one arm of the chair was the phone receiver. On the other were four segments of tangerine. He'd removed every scrap of pith from each one and placed the bald crescent pieces in a perfect line. Slowly he pushed the point of the pin against the turgid flesh of the nearest segment, enjoying the fraction of resistance before the skin punctured and the metal passed into the liquid-filled vessels on the other side. He withdrew the metal and watched the bead of moisture well up out of the tiny wound. Then he repeated the process on the other segments. Keys jangled outside and he quickly swept the pieces up, shoving them into his mouth before getting up with the phone in his hand. As his wife pushed open the door he waved to her while speaking into the dead receiver.

'Yeah, mate. No, the shoulder's feeling fine, a bit sore in the mornings, that's all. Another one? OK, I'll be there in a bit. OK. Cheers.' He pressed the hang-up button and replaced the phone on its cradle. 'That was old Clarke. Yet another frigging last-minute drop-off to Scotland. He wants me there as soon as possible.'

She struggled to manoeuvre the buggy through the door. 'Oh, well, it's all money in the bank, even if I never see you.'

'Yeah – that's the way to look at it.'

'Have you got enough time for some tea before you go? I've got some nice ham off the market. Extra lean.'

'Go on then – with those boiled potatoes in the fridge.'

'Of course, love.'

He sat back down on the sofa and started massaging his jaw, looking forward to the night ahead. His wife came into the room carrying Jasmine and placed her on the play mat in front of the television. Dave kept his eyes away from her as she started batting the objects hanging from the play gym arched over her head. A few minutes later his wife called, 'It's ready!'

They sat opposite each other at the kitchen table as Dave began hacking up the lump of cold ham on his plate.

'So where's tonight's delivery to?' she casually asked, sprinkling a large pinch of salt on to her potatoes.

'Fucking Dundee this time,' replied Dave through a mouthful of meat.

'Dundee?' Sally answered. 'I used to go there to see some cousins when I was a kid. That should take you about five hours each way. You'll have to bring me back some Dundee cake.'

'Sal – there'll be no shops open by the time I get up there,' he answered irritably.

'Mmm, you're right. Oh, tell you what, we were at Sam's this afternoon and Jasmine loved playing with Charlie's cars. Those big, chunky plastic ones. She especially liked his white van – wouldn't let go of it.'

'So?' asked Dave, not looking up. Wondering where this was leading.

'You could start taking her on deliveries when she's older. Sit her up in the front with you. I reckon she'd love it.'

The thought of his daughter swinging her feet in the footwell where the frightened eyes had been caused a wave of queasiness to stir in his stomach. He put down his knife and fork and looked at his watch.

'Better go,' he said, food making one cheek bulge outwards.

'You're not finishing your tea?' she asked.

'Chuck it in the fridge – I'll finish it when I get in,' he replied as he walked down the corridor. 'See you later!' he called and the door banged shut.

Slowly Sally cleared the table, then slumped down in front of the TV.

The phone rang ten minutes later.

'Hello, Sally, it's Bernard Clarke. Is Dave there, please?'

'He should be with you any minute. He set off from here a while ago.'

'To me?'

'Yeah – to collect the delivery for Dundee.'

'Dundee? I haven't rung him for any . . .' Suddenly he realised he was walking into something he didn't want to get involved in. 'Unless, um, it was Paul who rang him. I'll see when he gets here. Sorry to disturb you, Sal.' He was trying to get off the phone as fast as possible, but the cogs had already whirred in Sally's head.

'Hang on a minute,' she said. 'My fault, Bernard. I've mixed his nights up. He's minding the doors at some club in town tonight.'

'Oh well,' replied Bernard, sounding relieved. 'I've a last-minute one here, but it's only local. I can send it in a black cab.'

'Great. By the way, Bernard?'

'Yes?'

'Don't tell him I got his nights wrong, will you? He gets really wound up when I do my dizzy mum bit. All this looking after kids – it fills your head with cotton wool.'

'Don't worry, love, I won't breathe a word.'

'Thanks, Bernard.'

She pressed the hang-up button, fingers and toes tingling. Then she went into the kitchen and began looking through all the cupboards and drawers. Every time she found an old key she put it on the table and continued her search. An hour later she had rifled through the entire flat. Eleven keys lay on the table. She went next door and rang the bell.

'Hi, Edith. Could you do me a massive favour?' She looked back at her own open door. 'I've got a really urgent errand to run and Dave's off on a delivery. Is there any chance you could babysit Jasmine, just for an hour?'

The old lady smiled. ''Course, Sally. I'm only reading my book. I'll bring it through.'

Sally went back into her kitchen and pocketed all the keys. As she came back out on to the path, her neighbour was locking her front door. 'Thanks, Edith – you know where the tea and biscuits are,' said Sally 'I won't be long.'

Chapter 39
The Hunter

The full moon glowed in the night sky like an enormous hole into another world. Wisps of cloud scudded silently across it in the gentle breeze that must have been blowing hundreds of feet above. He'd parked his car in a layby about half a mile beyond the track. As he walked back along the road he checked over the contents of his pockets: torch, mobile phone (switched off), and Swiss Army knife. His plan was to locate the killer's car, break into it and actually make sure it did belong to the murderer, then puncture the tyres and phone for back-up from a hiding place nearby. He was well aware of the laws about citizen's arrest and, from what he remembered about the ones dealing with self-defence, knew that any blade larger than a penknife could sway any court case against him. Besides, hopefully he'd only have to use the knife on the car. At the top of the track he moved to the side and trod cautiously along the grass verge, stopping every so often. He couldn't help listening to the drone of the late-night motorway traffic going past in a futile effort to distinguish the put-put-put of his grandfather's ancient Morris Minor. Once he was certain no vehicle was parked on the track he climbed over the fence and quickly walked across the field. At the other side he looked around him in a vague attempt to see if anyone was watching and then lay down in the grass to wait.

Chapter 40
The Searcher

By the time he reached Eskwith his wrist was too painful to drive the extra mile to the stretch of track he'd parked on previously. So instead he pulled up at the top of the other track he'd seen when originally scouting the area over two months before. In a way it suited him better because he knew it was nearer to where the central reservation widened with the promise of extra finds. He slowed to a stop, and then reversed his car up the narrow lane with lights turned off, rolling slowly backwards to the bushes at the end. He pulled the handbrake, got out and opened the boot. As he changed into his overalls the screech-owl cried from close by, despairing and alone. Like a lost soul searching for something it could never find. Quickly he applied the grass snake's pattern to his hands and face.

At the edge of the field he looked down on to the patch of reservation he was aiming for. It was well over thirty yards wide and interspersed with numerous tall plants. A couple of hundred yards away he could just make out a cluster of small bushes growing right in the middle of the broad swathe of grass. He craned his head back and waited for the bank of cloud to slide across the sky and blot out the light from the full moon above. Half an hour later he was scuttling across the empty lanes.

Chapter 41
The Killer

The red glow worked its way through the line of traffic ahead like a Mexican wave. As it approached Dave replayed the conversation he'd had earlier in the kitchen with his wife. She thought it was five hours to Dundee and five back – that gave him an entire night to find some sport. And what happened? Fucking hours spent cruising the motorways and not a single breakdown.

The lights of the car in front finally lit up and grudgingly he pressed his own brakes too. His speed ebbed away to nothing. Searching the motorway lanes ahead, he looked for any sign of what had caused everyone to stop. He couldn't see a thing. A couple of minutes later they began edging slowly forward again and eventually he picked up enough speed to change out of first. He kept his eyes on the hard shoulder, aware of the full moon floating in the top of his vision, working his molars against the black rubber of the gum-shield he'd bought from the sports shop the day before, waiting to see what had caused the delay. Hoping it might have been fatal. Back up in fourth he realised he wasn't going to be treated to the sight of any wrecks. Bollocks, he cursed. Phantom traffic jams annoyed him even more than real ones.

With one hand on the wheel he reached down to the tape rack, careful to keep his eyes away from the passenger footwell where the frightened eyes had been, and slotted his only tape into the machine. He began to chew harder as Phil Collins started singing, 'I can feel it, coming in the air tonight'.

Her footsteps began to echo slightly as she entered the deserted courtyard of lock-ups. Weak light from a single lamp half lit the concrete around her. Sally shut her eyes and remembered the last time she'd been here. It had been a sunny afternoon, several years ago. Dave had just bought his van, promising an end to their money worries. They'd walked here together and proudly he'd shown her the blue garage door in the corner.

She opened her eyes to the darkness and looked to her left. There it was, now covered in graffiti. Taking a deep breath, she approached the expanse of metal. A padlock secured a thick strip of hinged iron to the door which, in turn, was embedded in the concrete with tamper-proof bolts. She reached into her pocket, took out the handful of keys, and crouched down.

The first one was far too small, so she selected the larger keys and began trying them. The first went in halfway but refused to turn. The second did the same, as did the third and fourth. The fifth slid in and turned easily. The U-shape of metal sprang upwards and Sally shook the padlock loose and folded the strip of metal back. Then she gripped the door handle with both hands and straightened her legs. The door rose with her, sliding up on its rollers into the roof.

The interior was pitch black. She took a couple of small steps forward, waving her outstretched arms before her. Her left hand brushed against a dangling string. She spread her fingers out wide and waited for it to swing back against them. Grasping it, she pulled downwards and the single bulb hanging inches in front of her face clicked on. The sudden glare made her squint, and through the blur of her eyelashes she surveyed the empty garage.

A shelf lined one wall, piled with old tins of paint and varnish. Brushes stood in empty glass jars; rubbish littered the floor. Collapsed burger restaurant cups with straws like broken antennae. Pages of crumpled newspaper. To her left, the tiny sink, the wall behind it speckled with dark brown dots. With her arms tightly crossed, she stepped into the centre of the floor, careful not to touch anything. Scrutinising everything. She saw the boiler suit in the corner, splashed with dirty water or oil. She stepped closer and her reflection was caught in the rust-stained mirror on the wardrobe door. She stared at the pale-faced woman with arms clutched in front of her and wondered just what she was looking for.

Her eyes shifted to the elaborately carved door handle, and using just her fingertips, she pulled at it gently. Wood grated stubbornly on wood. She pulled harder and suddenly the door swung open. She stared at the single object inside. A shoe. A little girl's red shoe with a daisy-shaped silver buckle on its side. Stepping backwards involuntarily, her head knocked into the naked bulb and her whole world lurched out of control.

Chapter 42
The Hunter

He lay there for over two hours. All the while the feeling that nothing was going to happen mounted. The moon had been buried by a thick bank of cloud an hour or so before, and he tried to work out if the darkness was to his advantage. Eventually he got up and returned to the track. At his feet he spotted a denser shape than the surrounding grass and squatted down. Cupping the end of his torch in his hand he turned it on and in the muted light examined the brittle cowpat. In its centre was the perfect imprint of a shoe. Andy knew he was close to finding him; he could sense it. Looking down to the end of the track he remembered the map, and how the track had re-emerged several fields further along.

Keeping on his side of the fence, he set off, skirting round the low hedge at the end and quickly trudging into the darkness beyond, eager to make it to the other track as fast as he could. Above the motorway's quiet hum all he could hear was the sound of his own breath and an occasional rustling behind him. At first the noise had bothered him and he kept on glancing around, half expecting to see something shadowing him. But after a while he worked out what it was: long strands of grass springing back up after he'd brushed against them. Twenty minutes later a low mass loomed up in front. Bushes. He altered his approach and went round their side. Behind the screen of foliage the red of a car's reflectors glinted dully in the night. He skirted carefully round the vehicle, noting that it was a light-coloured Datsun.

Chapter 43
The Searcher

He wormed his way forward, the squat bushes ahead filling up more and more of his vision. So far the stretch had been generous. A shuttlecock, a half-eaten stick of rock (Scarborough, the core had said), and the lower part of a lorry's radio aerial. The thin length of metal lay rigid in the leg pocket of his combats, and he realised it was forcing him to move lopsidedly. About twenty feet away from the bushes the cloying aroma of rotting flesh filled his nostrils. He welcomed the odour – it normally signified a promising find. Shutting his eyes, he used his sense of smell to direct him, homing in on the source like a baby animal blindly wriggling towards its mother's teat. The smell intensified into a stink as he felt the leaves of the first bush brushing his face. He worked his way to the side, but after a few seconds it grew fainter. He stopped and opened his eyes. Looking over one shoulder he stared at the shrubs: the smell was definitely coming from between them.

Chapter 44
The Killer

Shit. He realised it was time to start heading home. And he still hadn't passed a single breakdown. That made it a waste of time lying to Sal. Telling her he had been dropping off in Dundee so that, if he had found a bit of sport around Dover, she would have thought he was miles away in the other half of the country. He thought about when he might have another long trip. That was the problem with Bernard's last-minute deliveries: he could never plan ahead for them. Instead he slowly went over each detail of the last killing in his head, reliving the build-up to it and savouring the pleasure the act gave him. He snorted with derision as he remembered how the man had kept up his retching – even as he began swinging at the crown of his head with the monkey wrench.

He'd made his way up the M20, the M26 and round the M25 as usual. But with a jolt he found he had drifted, on autopilot, on to the M40. Ever since taking out the driver of the car with the little girl in, he'd been carefully avoiding this stretch of motorway. Unwelcome memories began to emerge and he tried to push them back with other thoughts, trivial considerations about his weight-training regime, the questions he got right on the quiz show last night. Anything at all. A sign for 'Services 3 miles' sped by; the same ones he'd used to change round the back of several weeks before. And he knew, to his dismay, that he was not only going to have to pass the spot where he'd snatched her, he was also going to have to pass the other spot a few miles further on. The one where, unable to take those staring eyes any longer, he'd pulled over, crushed the life out of her with his bare hands, wrapped the body in a blanket, run across the deserted motorway lanes and dumped it amongst some bushes on the central reservation.

Chapter 45
The Hunter

He'd got the Datsun's door open easily enough. But, aside from some empty shopping bags on the back seat, the inside of the car was empty. Nothing in the door's storage pockets to give the slightest clue about who the driver was. He opened the glove compartment and took out the half-empty packet of baby wipes. No documents or anything below. He sat in the driver's seat trying to imagine – trying to be – the driver. Guessing how he might operate. Remembering films he'd seen, he turned down the sun-visor – nothing again. Then he pulled up the lid of the ash tray. Used baby wipes were pushed inside. He teased one out and held it up in the darkness before him – he could just see that it was all discoloured, coated with something that didn't smell of shit. He bent forward into the footwell, brought the torch up against the material and turned it on – smears of green and black camouflage cream were sharply revealed to him. His heartbeat accelerated away.

This was it: he was in the killer's car. He'd found enough to get some support called out. He pulled his mobile from the breast pocket of his jacket and turned it on. As soon as the fluorescent screen settled down he began keying in the number for the desk at the motorway traffic police building. He pressed the last digit and the phone screen stood ready, asking him to 'Call?' Just as his forefinger was about to press 'OK' the phone beeped three times and the screen changed to 'New message. Listen now?' His finger pressed 'OK' and he was connected to the voicemail service. The digitised voice told him he had one new message, received today at 7.55 p.m., before his grandpa's recorded voice came on the line.

'Andrew? God knows why you carry that contraption around if you never have it switched on. Anyway I'm at home because the car won't start. Something up with the starter motor. So I'm not going anywhere tonight – probably set off tomorrow if the garage can get the parts. See you soon.'

Andy smiled into the black windscreen. His grandpa was safe. A great strain had been swept aside and the urgent need to call for help had vanished. Imagining the glory of cracking the case himself, he decided not to disable the car and call for help from a safe distance. Instead he would check the car boot for evidence of who the driver was. Putting the phone back in his pocket, he got out of the vehicle.

Skeletal toes poked out from between the blanket's folds. His eyes opened wide and saliva drooled from his parted lips where the torch was held between his teeth. He pulled at the blanket but it fell apart like soft tissue, revealing blackened feet. This, he instinctively knew, was the ultimate find: the pinnacle to his collection. He could taste the stench on the very roof of his mouth.

Immediately he wormed off towards the crash barrier to get the green plastic sheeting from the boot of his car. Recklessly abandoning his routine, he looked over the top of the strip of metal. Although there were no cars approaching on his side, vehicles were passing on the lanes across the reservation behind him. But he couldn't wait. Vaulting over the metal barrier, he sprinted across. As he did so the base of the aerial jabbed his leg painfully so, once on the grassy slope, he pulled it out.

As he jogged across the field a soft glow inside his car brought him to an abrupt halt. He watched from the darkness as the door opened and a shadowy figure got out, went round to the back of the car and crouched down at his boot. The torch glowed again. So finally here was one of those who observed him, who followed him, who tried to interfere. Only now it was his turn to observe. Silently he circled round and crept towards the rear of the vehicle. The person was intently picking at the lock, head bowed close to the metal. All his things were in the boot, including the plastic sheeting. Using the light that was escaping from the person's cupped hand to guide him, he approached ever nearer, filled with indecision about what he should do. The metallic rasps and ticks of whatever the person was using to pick the lock carried clearly in the still night air. Now, within two feet of the figure, he opened his mouth to draw in breath and as he did so the inner surface of his cheeks parted from the sides of his molars with a fleshy click.

The hands stopped their fiddling and the head began to turn.

His own arm swept in from the corner of his vision and he watched as the broken base of the aerial connected with the side of the person's neck before coming out, barely hindered, on the other side. With a curious rigidity, the person sat down heavily, dropping the torch and lifting his hands towards his neck. But his upper arms were somehow pinned so that only the elbows would bend. His fingers fluttered at shoulder level, just below the protruding lengths of metal. Blood shot with a faint hiss from one side, misting the registration plate in a fine spray.

With his foot he pushed the figure's chest and it fell stiffly away from the vehicle on to its back. He unlocked the boot, quickly pulled the plastic sheeting out and lowered the door back down. Then he turned off the person's torch and jogged back into the night, leaving the gurgling noises behind him.

Back on the other side of the field he hardly paused at the top of the slope – in the distance, lights were approaching but he raced down the incline anyway and dived over the crash barrier into the thick grass. Breathing heavily, he crawled back to the bushes, and once at the blanket unfolded the expanse of green plastic. On all fours he half rolled and half pushed the sodden lump on to it. Once it was in the middle he folded the material around it, the plastic crackling like an enormous sweet wrapper.

*

As the exit sign for the services approached he resisted the urge to pull in – knowing it only delayed the inevitable. What he really needed was a U-turn, so he could flee in the opposite direction. But the motorway forced him onward. Gritting his teeth against their black sheath, he gripped the steering wheel tighter.

The blood bubbled in the back of his throat as his hand, like a large hairless spider, walked slowly up his chest. Finally it settled on the hard object in his breast pocket and began pushing it out. Using just a fingertip and thumb he gained a precarious grip on its aerial, lifted it up and then repositioned it in his palm. He attempted to raise his hand to his face but his elbow would not move from his side. Instead he strained to look downwards and was just able to make out 'Call number?' on the lit screen. With his thumb he felt for the top right-hand button, pressed it and was connected to his old workplace. As soon as the tiny voice began to speak he coughed out a mouthful of blood and began rasping at the phone.

Dizzy with the enormity of his find, he got to his feet and strode quickly to the crash barrier. With some difficulty he got one of his legs over the metal while tenderly cradling the bundle in his arms. He half pirouetted and lifted his other leg over, stepped backwards on to the tarmac and turned around to start crossing the lanes. In his haste he'd totally forgotten to check for any lights and now, seeing the twinkling pair fast approaching, he lost his head and started to run. Immediately he stubbed a toe on a cat's eye and stumbled. Refusing to let go of the treasure clasped tightly to his chest, he fell heavily on to one knee.

As he passed the SOS phone where he snatched her, he put his foot even further down on the accelerator, desperate to get past the stretch as quickly as possible. The tape abruptly clicked to an end and the machine automatically switched to the radio. A static hiss immediately filled the cab and he glanced at the shattered panel venomously. The noise began to magnify in his head, escalating his feelings of sickness and panic. Oh God, he had to have music;

anything to break the tension cranking his brain ever tighter. He jabbed at the eject button and snatched at the tape as it slid out. Hurrying too much, his fumbling fingers dropped it and the tape fell on to the ridge separating his footwell from the passenger's. Jesus fucking Christ, he suddenly knew he was getting right to the spot where he'd pulled over and killed her. One hand on the steering wheel, he leant over and reached towards the tape lying balanced on the moulded plastic divide. Unable to see the road properly over the dashboard, his hand slipped on the wheel. As the van began to drift, the tyres on one side started to thump thump thump thump thump over the cat's eyes. The vibrations tipped the tape into the passenger footwell and a high-pitched whine started up in his throat.

He looked up and the lights were already much closer. Stranded between the middle and fast lanes, he struggled to his feet and took another step forward. But the lights moved with him, also heading towards the slow lane. The distance between him and the vehicle had now halved and even as he looked, it halved again. He stepped backwards and the two beams altered course towards him again, more sharply this time. Now it was frighteningly close. Hard tarmac surrounded him on every side and the van jinked slightly again, making it impossible to decide whether to dive forwards or backwards. And then he realised he had no time for either: he was going to be hit. He stood frozen, the glaring lights rushing directly at him.

He strained against the seat belt, and with eyes tightly shut lunged his hand into the darkness. Almost expecting it to be gripped by a little claw. The van lurched with the effort and he blindly readjusted the wheel. Just as his fingers grasped the tape and he began to straighten up, something slammed into the front corner of the van. The impact jarred the entire vehicle. He opened his eyes and hit the brakes simultaneously, looking in his rear-view mirror for the animal he'd hit. But, aside from a piece of white flipping over and over in the dark, the road behind was empty. He looked again at the pale rectangle turning end over end like a piece of cardboard in the wind and his stomach lurched as he realised it was his registration plate, ripped off in the collision. Finally it hit a snag on the road's surface and disappeared beneath the crash barrier on to the central reservation. Probably within feet of the girl's corpse. He couldn't risk leaving it so close to the scene of his crime. He pulled across the lanes, came to a halt on the hard shoulder and flicked his hazards on.

Gradually he became aware of a dimness above. The sky. He was on the central reservation again, this time lying on his back, grass pushing into his ear. From somewhere in the dark the protest of an engine sharply decelerating. He could feel nothing, sight and sound his only working senses. The engine's tone grew fainter, then faded into silence.

He lay still, barely breathing.

Letting his head fall a little more to the side, he could see the plastic sheeting and the greasy blanket with its pathetic contents curled across his forearm. He folded his chin in towards his chest and his head rose in what seemed to be a series of mechanical clicks so that, with each stage, a fraction more of his body was revealed to him. His waist was much wider and flatter. His hips were twisted around and his legs lay at an awkward angle to them, bent backwards towards his head, feet pointing in the wrong direction.

His head flopped back and refilling his lungs took more effort. He tried to flex his fingers but he couldn't sense any response. From far away, deep in the numbness of his back, a throbbing began. It had the same foreboding feel as heavy raindrops that announce the coming of a huge storm. His breathing was becoming shallow and too fast – something thick was gathering in his lungs, pushing out the air. Looking at the vague clouds above, he absently wondered if people would realise he hadn't actually killed the child. That he was merely collecting it. The waves of pain were now building in strength, flooding his stomach, lapping across his chest and throat, gradually submerging his head. Low over him the owl cut through the air, ghostly against the darker sky. With wings beating noiselessly, it disappeared into the crimson clouds closing in from the edges of his vision.

Manically chewing on the gum-shield, he leapt from the van and ran round it, clocking the dented front corner and crumpled bumper as he did so. With a stifled sob, he pulled open the sliding door. Then, with torch in hand, he jogged heavily back up the hard shoulder, warily eyeing the road for any approaching headlights. After about seventy metres he guessed he was about level with where his registration plate had bounced below the barrier. Something pale swooped silently over his head and vanished into the dark above the central reservation. He turned the torch on and shone it across the three empty lanes, but the beam only lit up the very outer edge of the grass bristling beneath the barrier. He knew he'd have to cross over and search for the piece of metal on the opposite side. Gulping back the urge to be sick, he ran across the tarmac and directed the powerful beam into the grass immediately beyond the barrier. Nothing. Slowly he went reluctantly on, playing the light further out into the grass. After a few steps he became aware of the bushes where he'd dumped her lurking in the darkness just ahead and, like a dog returning to its vomit, he couldn't resist flicking his wrist quickly towards them. The beam froze, illuminating a scene that went far beyond what his tortured mind could endure.

A misshapen emissary, emerged from the earth's very depths, stared back at him with white and sightless eyes. A snake-skinned ghoul, come to claim the child's rotten remains and drag them down somewhere unspeakable. And next to it, the girl he had strangled gazed directly at him from within her gathered shroud, the eyes dark and cold and empty.

A part of his brain finally snapped. He fell to his knees, and as he began howling at the hidden moon like a monster, the lights of the slowly approaching patrol car fell across his face.

Epilogue

With stiff arms Andy slowly folded the newspaper shut. 'I can't believe this. So he's – what's his name, Budgen? – he's been locked up already?'

'Detained under the Mental Health Act,' said his grandpa, leaning back in the chair at the side of Andy's bed. 'I'll bring you Sunday's papers. They had whole sections given over to it – including an artist's impression of the secure room he'll be in at Rampton. They had him sectioned within hours – the papers say all he's done is howl since your colleagues arrested him.'

'I could hear him from where I was lying,' said Andy, 'but I couldn't move a muscle.'

His grandpa's eyebrows buckled in sympathy. 'His wife called the police about the same time you rang for help.'

'His wife?'

'She had searched his lock-up and found the poor little girl's missing shoe hidden inside. Forensic teams went in and found evidence linking him to all six motorway murders. Blood-stained boiler suits, debris in the U-bend of the sink. And they have his van, of course. Some sort of murder weapon in his tool-kit, and the siren light he was using to fool broken-down drivers that he was a rescue vehicle.'

'So what about the person who stabbed me? The one who died on the central reservation next to the kid.'

'That's a mystery. The papers have gone into a frenzy trying to find out – but no one has a clue. Scotland Yard say they have a name, but they're not releasing it until his relatives have been traced. The Datsun's registration led them to an address in the city centre. Apparently his home was piled high with hundreds of plastic boxes containing things he'd collected from the central reservation.'

'Things?'

'The stuff you glimpse lying on the verge – debris, junk. Dead animals even. A police spokesman said they'd never seen anything like it – one paper said the whole house stank of whatever he was using to pickle his finds in.'

'Totally bizarre,' whispered Andy.

'You should read the editorial comment in that paper. It's asking how long Budgen could have gone on for if you hadn't made that phone call. Scotland Yard weren't even close to finding him. It compares it to the Yorkshire Ripper investigation – how many did he kill before they finally caught him? Fifteen? Sixteen?'

Andy waved a finger. 'Budgen's wife shopped him. It was only luck that I was there.'

'Well, that's not the way that lot out there see it,' his grandpa said, nodding towards the window. Andy pulled back the corner of the curtain and looked down at the gaggle of reporters gathered on the pavement six floors below.

'Were they really hassling you on the way in? It doesn't seem real,' he said, fingers going to the dressing at the side of his neck.

'You're quite a hero, Andy. It's no surprise they're desperate for information on you.'

There was a sharp rap on the door and instantly it swung open. 'Morning, Andy, how are the legs? Stiff from yesterday?' A young woman was backing into the room with a wheelchair. Instantly the old man was out of his seat and helping her with the door.

'Morning, Fiona. This is Alfred, my grandfather. Grandpa, this is Fiona, my own personal physio-terrorist.'

'Therapist, if you don't mind.' She smiled, swinging the wheelchair round and looking at Alfred. 'Hello, you must be very proud.'

'Not when he uses that sort of cheek – please excuse his lack of respect,' Alfred said with mock formality.

'She doesn't mind – she's a terrorist to herself too. She does triathlons,' Andy said.

'OK, OK – time we went down to the gym for your morning mobilisations,' Fiona quickly said, cutting off any further talk about herself. 'Now, are you OK getting your legs off the edge of the bed like yesterday?' she asked, manoeuvring the wheelchair up against the side of the bed and putting the brakes on.

Andy shuffled himself across, and with some effort swung his legs over the side. Then, with the physiotherapist supporting him, he shakily stood, turned slightly and sat down heavily in the wheelchair.

'Well done,' she said, clicking the brakes off with her foot.

'Are you coming to watch?' Andy asked his grandpa.

'May I?' he asked Fiona.

'Your shoes,' she said, looking at the brown slip-ons he was wearing. 'They're rubber-soled, aren't they?'

'Yes,' he replied.

'Then of course – you can hold the doors open for us.'

Together they headed down the corridor to the lift halfway along and descended to the first floor. At the end of the corridor they entered the gym area, the smell of polish scenting the air. Scattered around were some weight-machines, mini-trampolines, large balls and other rehabilitation equipment. Fiona wheeled Andy across the shiny wooden floor to a treatment bed and helped him on to it.

'Right, this morning we'll work on your quadriceps. First straighten your legs and press the backs of your knees into the bed.'

He did as instructed.

'Good. Now curl your left toes up so you can feel the tension in your calf muscle. OK, keeping your leg straight, I want you to raise it thirty degrees off the bed, and hold the position.'

Andy's teeth clenched, and a small muscle began straining out from the corner of his jaw. His foot lifted no more than three inches off the mattress and immediately his knee began to quiver. His hands gripped the sides of the bed as if it was swaying.

'Don't worry about lifting it any higher,' Fiona instructed. 'Just try and control the movement, and don't let your knee bend!'

Andy stared at his leg as it began to shake more violently.

'That's excellent,' encouraged Fiona. 'OK, now you can lower it slowly back down.'

Andy's breath hissed out in relief and his leg quickly dropped on to the mattress.

'Right, now for the other one.'

While massaging the aching muscles in his jaw, Andy glanced at his watching grandfather and said, 'See what I mean about physio-terrorist?'

The old man smiled and said, 'Do as she tells you.'

Andy went through the same exercise with his right leg, and then repeated the entire process once again.

The double doors creaked slightly as a police officer in full uniform tentatively stepped into the gym. All three looked across at him. 'Hello.' He coughed awkwardly. 'Could I interrupt?'

Fiona pointed to his shoes. 'You're welcome to talk with Andy, but you'll have to leave your shoes outside. They'll mark the floor.'

'Yes. Yes, of course,' he replied, hurriedly untying his laces and placing the immaculate black leather shoes outside the door. They all noticed the small hole in his left sock. Taking slightly shorter steps than normal to prevent himself from slipping, the Inspector walked silently across the floor. He nodded to the physio and then to Alfred. 'Hello, you must be Constable Seer's grandfather. I'm his senior officer, Inspector Marsh.'

'Pleased to meet you,' said Alfred, shaking his hand.

'So,' said Inspector Marsh, addressing Fiona, 'how's he doing?'

'Extremely well,' she replied, not looking up from bending Andy's foot backwards. 'Fortunately the aerial glanced off his cervical vertebrae without causing much nerve damage. Its immediate effect was to cause his muscles to spasm, locking his arms at his sides. What little nerve damage he sustained is causing numbness in his lower legs. But,' and she looked directly at Andy, 'if he sticks to his exercises, he should be fully fit in a matter of months.'

'That's most encouraging,' said Marsh. 'And Dr Vashnay informs me your sleep cycle is reasserting itself too,' he continued, now looking at Andy.

'I think so – the last couple of nights have been especially good. But that could be the painkillers.' Andy smiled, and Marsh, taking his cue from the younger man, quickly grinned too.

'Well, I'm delighted to say we're ready and waiting for you to resume your attachment with us – all the lads send their regards.'

'All?' asked Andy, propping himself up on his elbows.

Marsh glanced uneasily at Fiona and Alfred.

'Fiona, could we just have two minutes, please?' asked Andy.

'Yup – I'll get a walking frame.' Briskly she set off across the floor, trainers squeaking with every step.

Andy looked expectantly at his Inspector who, with another quick glance at Alfred, quietly said, 'Walker's gone. We agreed it best he should leave immediately – so he cleared his locker and desk during the graveyard shift. I won't lie to you, Andrew, with the killer found it serves no purpose stringing up Walker. A state pension is punishment enough without prosecution too. That would only stir up a stink for all of us.'

He waited nervously for Andy's answer.

'That's fine by me – I don't want anything more to do with him,' he replied.

His boss's shoulders relaxed a fraction as the squeak of Fiona's trainers returned. 'I'm glad you agree,' he said. Then, with his voice at a normal level again, 'Well, I won't hold you up any longer, and I look forward to seeing you soon.' Quickly he shook Alfred's hand and said to Fiona, 'You get this young man fit. We need him back.' He stepped across the gym and halfway out of the door called back, 'By the way, Constable Seer, just let me know when you want to take your advanced driving course – you have a place booked for whenever you want it.'

Andy waved a hand and said, 'As soon as possible, sir.' The door swung shut.

'Right,' said Fiona. 'Now he's finished licking your arse, can we get some work done?' Andy and Alfred both laughed as she positioned the frame by the bed. Then, with her help, Andy slowly stood.

'OK, one step at a time and take it very slowly,' she instructed as Andy edged the frame forward. Laboriously he slid his left foot then his right across the smooth floor. 'That's good, keep it going,' Fiona encouraged.

Andy looked up into his grandpa's delighted eyes. The old man broke into an enormous smile and with pride choking his voice whispered, 'Remember what she said, son. One step at a time. One step at a time.'

Acknowledgements

My gratitude to Emma for her early criticism and encouragement, Vanessa for her information about the police, Paul Oldbury for his inside guide to the motorway traffic police, Julia, Helenka and Ros for spotting me in the slush pile and the team at Random House for all their enthusiasm.